And then, at last, he said, "And now, it's with great pleasure and sincere admiration that I introduce to you… Mitch Valentine."

There was roaring. It was partly the applause and it was partly the blood spurting so fast through her veins. It made a rushing in her ears.

A tall, broad-shouldered man in a dark suit with a snow-white shirt and a lustrous blue tie strode confidently across the stage. She thought, *Chestnut-brown hair, like Michael's.*

He stepped up to the podium under the hard gleam of the spotlight. And he spoke. "Thank you, Dr. Benson. I'll do my best to live up to that glowing introduction."

She'd known for certain in her mind when he faced the audience, but when he spoke, she knew in her heart.

The final shreds of her doubt unraveled and dropped away.

Kelly *knew.*

He was Mic ter's father at last

Dear Reader,

We all remember our first love. Nothing like it. Passionate and all-consuming, young love makes us swear to give each other everything, to be together for eternity.

But the world so often gets in the way. We are forced to break our first-love vows.

So it was for Kelly Bravo and Michael Vakulic. They loved with all their young hearts—and lost each other too soon.

And now, a decade later, Michael is back. And Kelly braces herself to tell him that he left more than his first love behind when he vanished from her life all those years ago.

As you might imagine, it's a Valentine's Day surprise like no other.

Yours always,

Christine Rimmer

CHRISTINE RIMMER

VALENTINE'S SECRET CHILD

SPECIAL EDITION®

Published by Silhouette Books

America's Publisher of Contemporary Romance

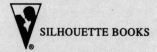

SILHOUETTE BOOKS

ISBN-13: 978-0-373-24879-7
ISBN-10:   0-373-24879-2

VALENTINE'S SECRET CHILD

Visit Silhouette Books at www.eHarlequin.com

Printed in U.S.A.

CHRISTINE RIMMER

came to her profession the long way around. Before settling down to write about the magic of romance, she'd been everything, including an actress, a salesclerk and a waitress. Now that she's finally found work that suits her perfectly, she insists she never had a problem keeping a job—she was merely gaining "life experience" for her future as a novelist. Christine is grateful not only for the joy she finds in writing, but for what waits when the day's work is through: a man she loves, who loves her right back, and the privilege of watching their children grow and change day to day. She lives with her family in Oklahoma. Visit Christine at her new home on the Web at www.christinerimmer.com.

For Leena Hyat,
brilliant and tireless advocate
for so many romance authors.
Lee, your warmth and thoughtfulness
mean so much!

Chapter One

"Valentine." Renata Thompson sighed. Dramatically. "Won't you be mine?"

Kelly Bravo glanced over her shoulder, coffeepot in hand. "Doubtful."

Renata let out a laugh. "Not a problem. You may be the boss, but you're just not my type."

Kelly filled her mug and put the pot back on the warming plate. She took the chair across from Renata. "So, then. Who's your valentine?"

"His *name* is Valentine. *Mitch* Valentine." Renata had the *Sacramento Bee* spread open on the round breakroom table. She pointed a slim brown finger at a publicity headshot of some guy. Kelly glanced at it without really looking, shrugged and sipped her coffee.

"You must have heard of him," Renata insisted. "Guy has billions. Owns a bunch of companies. Started from zip. Now he's written a book. *Making it Happen: Change Your Mind, Transform Your Life.*"

Kelly sipped again. "Sounds…uplifting. But, no. Sorry. The name's not ringing a bell."

Renata's mug said Shrink. She grabbed it and took a swig of the murky breakroom brew. "He's speaking at Valley University tonight. I may have to go. Whether he changes my life or not, he is superhot. And as rich as they come. Hot and rich. Does it get any better?"

"Well, now." Kelly raised her own mug high. "A good sense of humor. Gotta have that."

"Honey, if he's rich and hot, he doesn't need to make me laugh. We'll spend our lives shopping— and having sex."

"I am shocked, I tell you." Kelly put on her most disapproving frown. "Shocked."

Renata spun the paper around and slid it across to Kelly's side of the table. "Look." She plunked her finger down hard right above the photo of Mr. Hot-and-Rich. "Tell me you'd pass up a chance with *that.*"

Kelly groaned. "Sorry. Not interested. I'm a single mom with a full-time job. I don't have time to go chasing after some Tony Robbins wanna-be."

"The eyes alone. In-tense. *Look.*"

So Kelly looked. "Oh, my. He's very…" The words trailed off. "Not possible," she heard herself whisper.

"'Scuse me?"

But Kelly didn't answer. She stared at the photo and couldn't believe what she was seeing.

From somewhere far, far away Renata was asking, "Kelly? Kelly, are you all right?"

She was not all right. Not in the least. Because she knew those eyes. That mouth. That straight slash of brow…

Michael.

He looked…older.

But of course he would, wouldn't he? It *had* been a decade, after all.

His face, once hollow-cheeked, had filled out. His shoulders—what she could see of them— were broader. Much broader. He seemed, in the photo, so…confident. This man looked as if he was ready to take on the world, a mover and shaker if ever there was one, the polar opposite of the boy she had loved.

But still. She would know those eyes and that mouth anywhere. Her thin, withdrawn video-game-obsessed high-school sweetheart, Michael Vakulic, had become someone named Mitch Valentine.

"God. Kelly. Are you—"

"Fine." Kelly forced herself to lift her head and aim a smile at the dark, exotic face across the table. "I'm fine." She played it light, pretended to fan herself. "Whew. You're right. The guy is hot."

Renata's worried frown faded. "Told you so." Now she was looking exceedingly smug. She reached to take the paper back.

But before she completed the action, Carol Pace, the center's business manager, appeared in the open doorway. "Renata. I need the file on the J. Carera family."

Renata was one of the four family counselors Kelly had on staff at Sacramento County Family Crisis Center. The woman was amazing with families in trouble, but not so hot at keeping on top of her paperwork. "It should be there. Filed under *C*."

"No kidding. Not there."

"All right, all right. I'm coming…" Shaking her curly head, Renata got up and followed Carol out.

There was no one else in the breakroom. Kelly had never been so grateful to be left alone in her life.

Ordering her hands to stop shaking, she folded the paper with Michael's picture on it, grabbed her coffee and stood on shaky legs. Once upright, she raced out the door and down the hall, sloshing coffee as she went.

At last, she reached her corner office. She darted

inside, then stuck the paper under her arm to free a hand so she could close the door and turn the lock.

The lock clicked shut. She leaned her forehead against the doorframe and whispered desperately, "It can't be him, no way it's him...."

Her heart was galloping like a hundred wild horses. She sucked in a long breath, let it out with agonized slowness and ordered her pulse to stop pounding so loud she couldn't hear herself think.

God. Her whole body was shaking. She'd splashed coffee on the back of her hand—and her shoes, as well.

With another deep breath, she pushed off from the door, turned and made herself walk to her desk. She set her coffee cup on the stone coaster, where her nine-year-old daughter, DeDe, had personally painted a stick-figure deer along with the words *Mommy, you're a dear* in shiny pink letters.

The newspaper slid out from under her arm and flopped to the floor. Swearing under her breath, she grabbed it up, slapped it down on the desk and whipped out a few tissues from the box by her computer monitor.

She wiped the coffee off the back of her hand and then slipped off one tan suede shoe and then the other, to try and get the coffee off of them. Were they ruined? She'd take a brush to them when she got home. But at the moment, a wrecked pair of shoes was the least of her problems.

Michael. Oh, God. Michael...

Her phone rang. She punched Hold without picking up, then buzzed the receptionist. "Melinda, I'm in the middle of something here." Well, it was true. And it was something big—even if it wasn't the least work-related. "Could you take that call for me and get a message? And hold my calls until further notice... Yes. Terrific. Thanks." She hung up and dropped into her swivel chair.

The section of paper was right there on the desk pad in front of her, folded and folded again, the pages slightly disarranged now....

Gripping the chair arms in white-knuckled hands and glaring at the folded paper, Kelly swung the chair sharply back and forth. Such a seemingly harmless thing. The *Sacramento Bee* for Tuesday, February 13th. Innocuous. Mundane.

Yet it threatened to change her life and the life of her only child. Forever.

DeDe, in pink tights and a tutu, beamed at her from the picture on the corner of her desk. That one had been taken at one of her dance recitals last fall. Next to it, there was one of DeDe and Candy, the ancient black mutt that had showed up on their doorstep five years before and swiftly become one of the family. DeDe, seven at the time the picture was taken, had her arms around the dog's neck. She was smiling wide, proudly displaying the gap where she'd lost two front baby teeth. There were others pictures of DeDe, on the bookcase, as well as on the credenza. Two of them showed Kelly and DeDe together, one was of DeDe with her uncle Tanner and another of DeDe, Kelly, Tanner—and Hayley, who was Kelly and Tanner's long-lost sister. They'd found Hayley just that previous June....

Kelly closed her eyes, sucked air through her nose. She could look at all her office pictures again. And again. A thousand times. But eventually, she'd have to open that paper. There was, in the end, no escaping the image there. The truth had to be faced.

With swift, determined movements, she hauled her chair in close to the desk and spread the paper wide.

And there he was again. Michael.

Older, bigger, stronger, more confident, more... everything. But still. It was Michael. She was certain.

She touched the face in the picture, closed her eyes, whispered fervently, like a prayer, "I tried, I swear. I tried to find you. I *knew* I would find you. At first. But I never did. And somehow, over the years... Oh, God. I'm so sorry. But I had started to think it was never going to happen...."

She was sagging again, kind of crumpling into herself. Not good. She needed to sit tall. Once more, she drew herself up. She reached for the phone and dialed her brother's cell.

Tanner answered on the second ring. "Tanner Bravo." Tanner was a private investigator. He owned his own detective service, Dark Horse Investigations. He'd been looking for Michael all along, with no luck.

"It's me." Her voice came out sounding absurdly small.

"Kell. You okay?"

"I'm fine."

"You sound—"

"I'm fine," she insisted. "Look. I was wondering. Do you think you could come over tonight, keep an eye on DeDe for a couple of hours?"

"Got a hot date?" Tanner was forever teasing her about her dateless state. As a rule, she teased him right back, razzed him that *he* ought to find someone nice and settle down.

Right now, though, she didn't feel much like teasing. "Har-har. And no. It's not a date. There's this guy speaking at Valley U. A motivational thing…"

"You need motivating?"

"One of the counselors here at the center recommended him." Well. Renata *had* recommended him. Though not exactly for his skills as a speaker.

"Do I get a free meal out of it?"

"Slow-cooker pot roast. Biscuits. For dessert, vanilla ice cream and oatmeal-raisin cookies."

"Right answer. You're in luck. I don't have anything going on after five. What time d'you need me?"

She scanned the article in front of her, looking for a time. "Uh, the program starts at seven-thirty. Come at six. We'll eat before I go. I should be home by ten at the latest."

He agreed he'd be there and they said goodbye.

She hung up feeling guilty for not telling him that the motivational speaker just happened to be Michael.

But no. She wasn't absolutely sure the man was Michael, not yet. She needed to see him in person first, needed to be beyond-a-doubt certain about this before she got everyone all stirred up.

Mitch Valentine was speaking in the sociology center, an auditorium called Delta Hall. The hall had theater-style seating for at least a thousand and when Kelly arrived at twenty after seven, a good half of the seats were taken.

Quite a crowd for a self-help speaker on a Tuesday night. Was Renata here somewhere? Kelly hoped not. The situation was tough enough. She didn't need the added stress of trying to behave normally for one of her colleagues.

Kelly dithered—upstairs or down? Front, center or at the rear? More people filed in around her.

Finally, frazzled to no end, a bundle of nerves at the prospect that Michael might be in the same building with her and in ten minutes she would see him in the flesh, she chose a seat about a third of the way up from the stage. Close enough that she should be able to tell if the man named Mitch Valentine was actually Michael.

And far enough back that she doubted he would pick her out of the crowd—again, if he did turn out to be Michael. And if he remembered her.

It *was* possible, after all, that he *was* Michael and he'd totally forgotten he was ever passionately, possessively in love with a girl named Kelly. He'd clearly moved on. And he didn't know about DeDe. Yet.

What was there to hold him to the memory of those long-ago days?

Next to her, a college-age girl wearing a shearling jacket and boots that looked as if they belonged on an Eskimo, giggled and turned to the girl on her other side. "Hottie. I'm so not kidding. Fully doable. You should have gone to the reception before. He shook my hand. God. Those eyes. That voice. I think I came. And you know how I feel about the damn required lectures. But here I am. And you don't hear me complaining…."

Her girlfriend was not impressed. "I'll wait 'til I see him. And I still hate these lectures."

"Trust me," said the girl in the Eskimo boots. "You get a look at him, you'll change your mind."

The two put their heads together and started whispering.

Kelly tuned them out. Michael had always had a fine, deep voice and beautiful eyes. Most people hadn't noticed, back then. They saw a skinny, withdrawn teenager and never looked beyond that.

So was that more proof that she'd found him, at last?

Wait, the voice of caution warned. *Get a look at him. You'll know soon enough.*

It was warm in the hall and her nerves weren't helping her cool down any. She wiggled out of her winter coat and draped it over the back of her chair.

By the time she faced front again, the lights were dimming over the seats—and getting brighter on the stage, brightest of all on the podium, center stage. A man came striding out of the wings: tall, thin, gray hair...

Not Michael. Or even the man she suspected might be Michael.

The gray-haired man stepped up to the podium to polite applause. He introduced himself as the head of the sociology department and then launched into a glowing introduction of the evening's guest speaker.

Most of it had been in the paper that morning.

"Mitch Valentine is living, breathing proof that the American Dream really can come true. At nineteen, he designed his first video game. How many of you ever played DeathKnot or Midnight Destroyer?" Hands went up all over the hall. The professor smiled. "From there, he moved into software development, then created a job-search engine for students. Many of you here tonight have or will use FirstJob.com before you send out those resumes. From there, Mitch moved into desktop publishing. Now, at twenty-eight, he owns two publicly traded companies with headquarters in Dallas and in Los Angeles. And he's written a book about how he did it."

Her heart was beating too fast again. *Michael would be twenty-eight now....*

And the video games. They hadn't mentioned the video games in the paper, had they?

The department head was still talking. About how Mitch Valentine had started from nothing, lived on the streets of Dallas, turned his life around. How he had no formal education beyond a high-school diploma, and yet...look at the man today.

And then, at last, he said, "And now, it's with great pleasure and sincere admiration that I introduce to you...Mitch Valentine."

There was a roar. It was partly the applause and it was partly the blood spurting so fast through her veins, it made a rushing in her ears.

A tall, broad-shouldered man in a dark suit with a snow-white shirt and a lustrous blue tie strode confidently across the stage. She thought, *Chestnut-brown hair, like Michael's…*

He stepped up to the podium under the hard gleam of the spotlight. And he spoke.

"Thank you, Dr. Benson. I'll do my best to live up to that glowing introduction…."

He spoke.

She'd known for certain in her mind when he faced the audience, but when he spoke, she knew in her heart.

The final shreds of her doubt unraveled and dropped away.

Kelly *knew.*

He was Michael. She had found her daughter's father, at last.

Chapter Two

Mitch Valentine, who had once been Michael Vakulic, talked for over an hour, without notes. He rarely stood still. Instead, he paced back and forth in front of the podium, pausing now and then to turn his arresting gaze on the audience as he emphasized a certain point. He wore one of those little portable mikes that hooked over his right ear, with a thin mouthpiece curving over his cheek, so his voice was crystal clear even though he spoke in a conversational tone.

He talked about starting from nothing. About never giving up. About making the impossible into the possible. About translating dreams into reality, about goals, about what gets in the way of getting what we want.

He was funny and he was brilliant and he was inspiring. And he had that audience in the palm of his hand. Even Kelly, though hardly in a receptive frame of mind, was impressed. Hey, she just might have learned something under different circumstances.

That night, though, she sat there wide-eyed, her heart in her throat, images of the Michael she had known back then popping in and out of her stunned mind, warring with the reality of Mitch Valentine now.

Up on the stage, the broad-shouldered man in the designer suit said, "Set yourself up in opposition, and where does all your energy go? Exactly. Into the fight—into *opposing*. But set yourself up in *cooperation,* and something altogether different occurs...."

In her mind's eye, she saw Michael, *her* Michael, in a cheap white T-shirt and battered, sagging jeans, his arms like two sticks, his hair shoulder length and stringy. His dark, hazel eyes were shining and his thin face seemed to glow from within.

He said, *"I love you, Kelly. You're everything to me. I'll always take care of you. It's you and me against the rest of them...."*

Mitch Valentine said, "Ultimatums? I believe they're the simplest way to sabotage yourself, to make certain you get the short end of the stick instead of what you want...."

And she remembered Michael the day he made her choose. *"Me and you, Kelly. Don't you remember? It was supposed to be me and you, always. If you leave with him, it's over. So make a choice. Him. Or me."*

"But Michael, he's my brother...."

"Him or me, damn you. Just make a choice."

And so it went the whole time Mitch Valentine spoke.

She tried to put aside her fears as to how finding Michael would change her life—and her daughter's life—irrevocably. She tried to focus her attention on the man Michael had become. And then that man would say something else to send her spinning back in time.

Past. Present. Future: what *had* happened, what was happening this moment, what might happen next...

The present was unbearable, the past so hard to face. And the unknowable future? It seemed to bear down on her like an avalanche, like an asteroid on a collision course with the world she had created for herself and her child....

When the speech ended, Mitch Valentine took questions.

That went on for half an hour.

Finally, he thanked everyone and said he'd be signing his new book at the campus bookstore the next day, between three and five. The applause was protracted and enthusiastic. The house lights got brighter as the stage lights dimmed. Most of the audience headed for the exits, but fifty or sixty of them rushed onstage.

Another twenty minutes dragged by as Michael—correction: Mitch—accepted praise and shook hands. Kelly waited in her seat until only a few students remained.

When all but those last stragglers had headed for the doors, she made herself rise and put on her coat. Her heart hammering in her ears as it had been doing for most of the night, she slid out into the aisle and strode purposefully down front. There were stairs leading up to the stage on either side. She took the set to the left.

Once up there, she hung back, until the final student had finished gushing and shaking the speaker's hand.

The student turned to go. The man who had once been Michael glanced toward Kelly where she hovered on the edge of the stage. He smiled.

Her heart stopped racing. It seemed to expand in her chest. A shiver went through her at the same time as heat bloomed in her midsection. This was really happening, the impossible moment was upon her, at last.

He asked, "Kelly?"

Sweet relief poured through her. It mattered a whole lot, that he remembered. That he recognized her. She gulped and nodded.

He started toward her, so big and strong and... imposing. Imagine. *Her* Michael had grown up to be imposing.

He stood in front of her. She looked up into those velvety eyes that looked deep brown in some lights, and in others, showed glints of green: Michael's eyes. He said, "I have to admit, I kind of wondered if you might be here, if you might have come back to Sacramento...."

When they split up, she'd moved to Fresno, where Tanner was living and working when he finally got their mother to admit he had a sister. Tanner was twenty-one at the time and the court allowed him custody, once Kelly stood up before a judge and declared that she wanted to live with her brother.

She gulped in air and made herself explain. "My mom got sick again, a year after Tanner came for me. She needed us. And I wanted to go to Sac State anyway...."

He smiled again. He had the most beautiful smile. But then, so had Michael, though his smiles were rare. "Let me guess. You got a full scholarship?"

"That's right."

"I knew you would. And you've been here in Sacramento ever since?"

"Yes, I...have a house. A job I love. An old black dog." *And a daughter. Your daughter...*

"Mitch. Ready?" said a voice from behind her. A glance over her shoulder showed her that the gray-haired professor waited in the wings.

Mitch gave him the high sign. "Be right there, Robert."

She faced Mitch again. "I guess you have to go, but..." What to say next? It seemed all wrong to just dump the news on him without preamble, right there on that darkened stage.

"Listen." He looked at her so intently, scanning her face in a way that seemed both eager and hungry at once. A funny thrill skittered through her. And the warmth in her stomach seemed to expand outward, to radiate all through her.

My God. I'm attracted to him—and he feels it, too....

After all these years. Who knew? He'd changed so much. And then there was DeDe. God. What would he do when she told him about DeDe?

He said, "I believe in keeping it simple and direct."

"Oh. Yes. I prefer that, too." But obviously not *that* direct. Or she would have told him already that he was a dad.

No. Really. Bad idea, to just blurt it out, out of

nowhere, with that professor lurking behind them, waiting to lead Mitch off to who knew where.

Mitch asked, "Are you married? Engaged? With someone special?"

A short burst of surprised laughter escaped her. "Well, that *was* simple and direct. And the answers are no, no. And no."

"Perfect."

She actually found herself teasing him. "Which *no* do you mean?"

"All of them." The air seemed to crackle around them. With energy. With…heat. He said, "I've got this faculty party I have to be at right now, but I'm in town 'til Thursday morning. How about dinner tomorrow night?"

Tomorrow was Valentine's Day. How weird was that? To go out with her child's father, whose name was now Valentine…on Valentine's Day?

Weirdness aside, though, dinner would work. Just the two of them, sharing a table in a quiet restaurant. It would be a good opportunity—if there was such a thing—to break the news.

He said, "You're taking too long to answer. I'm getting worried you'll say no again—this time to me."

Her cheeks felt too warm. She couldn't resist. "No." She paused just long enough for him to look disappointed. Then she added, "I'm not saying no."

He laughed, then. "Seven?"

"Fine." She hurried right on, before he could suggest that he would pick her up. "I'll meet you at the restaurant, if that's all right?"

"However you want it."

She'd put a business card in her pocket, ready for this moment. "Here's my work number and my cell, just in case…" Their fingers touched in the space between them. So strange. After all these years, the two of them, standing here. Breathing the same air, his hand brushing hers…

His skin was warm. Dry. And only slightly rougher than her own.

He produced a card and handed it over. It was thick vellum, green with black lettering, a personal card, just his name and a couple of phone numbers.

"If you need to call, use the first number," he said. "It's my cell."

"All right."

"Shall I ask around, get some recommendations for the right restaurant, or do you know where you'd like to eat?"

She named a place in midtown, on 28th Street. "It's quiet there," she said. "And the food's good."

"I remember it," he said. "A Sacramento land-mark. Though we never could afford to eat there, back when…" The place wasn't terribly expensive, but for two kids with no money, it had seemed so— And Dr. Benson must be getting impatient, because

Mitch was glancing over her shoulder and nodding. "Right there…"

She stepped back. "I'll let you go then."

"Until tomorrow…"

"Seven. I'll be there."

Tanner was stretched out on the couch in the family room at the back of the house, channel-surfing, when Kelly got home. He turned off the TV and reached over to set the remote on the coffee table when she came in through the dining room.

He didn't get up right away, but braced his right arm behind his head and regarded her through lazy, dark brown eyes. "You're late. I was practically asleep."

"At twenty after ten? You know you never went to sleep this early in your life."

He sat up then, kind of stiffly. He'd been in a car accident six weeks before and had only gotten the casts off his left arm and leg a few days ago. A week or two more, his doctors said, and even the residual stiffness should disappear. He yawned. "Good speech?"

"Excellent."

"What was that name again?"

"Mitch Valentine."

He shrugged. "Never heard of him."

She only smiled. She'd made up her mind on the drive home not to tell Tanner that she'd found

Michael at last until *after* she'd managed to tell Mitch about DeDe. It seemed right that she should come clean with Mitch, first and foremost.

But she and her brother were very close. Guilt nagged her, to hold out on him this way.

He was frowning. "Okay, what's going on?"

And she couldn't go through with it, couldn't hold the truth back. Not from Tanner, who was her beloved big brother, her rock, the first one to show her what it could be to have a real family. She came and sat beside him and took his hand. "Is DeDe asleep?" She pitched her voice barely above a whisper.

His brow crinkled with concern. "She went to bed at nine. I checked on her about fifteen minutes ago. Dead to the world."

"Good. I…"

"God, Kell. What?"

"Mitch Valentine? The guy who was speaking to-night?"

"Yeah?"

"He's Michael."

He looked every bit as stunned as she felt. "What the hell?"

"It's true. Oh, Tanner. I've found Michael. At last…"

He let go of her hand. "Are you sure?"

Kelly bobbed her head up and down. "Oh, yeah. He's Michael, though he's changed a lot. You know how thin he was? Not anymore. He's…buffed up. And he's wealthy. Owns a couple of companies and he's written a book about how he turned his life around."

Tanner said patiently, "Kell. Listen. How can you be certain this guy is the kid you knew in high school?"

"What do you mean? I saw him, face-to-face. I talked to him."

"Tonight?"

"Yes. I waited around after he spoke. The minute he saw me, he recognized me, too."

"You really are certain."

"I am. You wait. You'll see. He's changed, yes, but he's still Michael."

"Mitch Valentine. That's the name he goes by now?"

"That's right."

"What's going on with that? Why did he change his name?" Tanner wore his most unreadable expression. Kelly knew what that look meant. He'd be burning the midnight oil on the Internet tonight, using the various tools at his disposal as a P.I. to find out everything he could about the man named Valentine.

"Oh, Tanner. Come on. Don't be so suspicious. I know you didn't like him, but—"

"Sorry. I *am* suspicious. The guy vanishes into

thin air. For ten years. And now he's back and rich and buffed up—living under an assumed name?"

"Please. I left him and his mother died. A one-two punch. He took off, started over. And people do change their names, you know. It's not as though it's a crime."

"But he didn't tell you why he did it."

"We talked for like, three minutes. There wasn't time. Tomorrow, I'll find out more."

"Tomorrow?"

"We're meeting for dinner. He's leaving town Thursday."

"To go where?"

"Haven't a clue. All I know is somehow I have to get up the nerve to tell him he's got a daughter."

"And you want me to watch DeDe again, while you talk to him?"

"If you can…"

He was silent for a moment, then he nodded. "Of course I can."

"Thank you."

"When will you tell *her?*"

"Soon. After I tell *him.* I need to see how he takes it. I've waited so long to find him." She shook her head. "And now I have, I have no idea how he's going to react to this. I just…I don't know. He's the same, but so different. If that makes any sense at all."

Tanner reached for her hand again. She gave it. He squeezed her fingers. "Damn. Not easy, huh?"

She let herself sag against him. "I can hardly believe this is happening."

"Yeah. I hear you. Me, neither."

She rested her head on his broad shoulder. "Tanner?"

"Huh?"

"At least we finally found him."

"Right." Something in his tone alerted her.

She straightened so she could see his face. "Please. Don't feel bad because you weren't the one who found him. I know you did everything you could. I always felt so awful for you. So many times I've asked you how the hunt was going. And each time you had to tell me you had nothing. I know how much you hated that."

His dark gaze slid away, but only for a second or two. Then he looked straight at her again. "Listen. You found the guy. That's what matters."

She smiled then, in spite of her apprehensions. "Yeah. It's happened, after so many years I'd begun to wonder if it ever would. Now I have to tell him that he's got a daughter, that he's missed the first nine years of her life. I have the strangest feeling he's not going to take that especially well."

Tanner scowled. "He's the one who turned his back on you—and then ran away without leaving a clue as to where he'd gone. There's no way he can expect you to have found him. He didn't even keep the same name."

"Tanner. Chill. Really, maybe I'm worrying over nothing. It's not as if he was a mixed-up teenager anymore. He was perfectly charming. Sophisticated. With a great sense of humor…"

"Now I know for sure you've got the wrong guy."

"Oh, stop." She slapped him playfully on the arm and mentally added, *He's also sexy. Very, very sexy.* She thought about the way Mitch had looked at her, the heat in those beautiful eyes, and suppressed a dreamy sigh.

Tanner grumbled some more. "The man had damn well better watch himself, that's all."

"Spoken like my own wonderful, protective big brother—and do not get yourself all worked up. I mean it. That's an order."

"Hell. All right." He peered more closely at her. "You gonna be okay?"

"Oh, I hope so. I truly do."

Chapter Three

Mitch got to the restaurant early. He'd called ahead and reserved a quiet corner table, but he wanted time to check it out personally before Kelly arrived, to make sure it was everything the guy who took his reservation had promised.

The place was nice. Kind of cozy. With an inviting bar, dimly lit, on one side, and a quiet dining room on the other. This time of year, the famous patio area was closed. But Mitch wasn't complaining. The table he'd reserved was just as he'd hoped, tucked away in a corner under a muted overhead light. On the snowy-white linen tablecloth, there was a curvy candle, of clear glass, the kind that burned oil. And a white magnolia blossom floated in a square crystal vase.

"Thank you. It's just right," he told the host as he pressed a fifty into the man's palm. He took the chair with a clear view of the entrance and ordered Tanqueray on the rocks. When the drink came, he sipped it slowly and suppressed an ironic smile.

Crystal, his friend in L.A. who insisted on telling people he was her brother, would have a good laugh on him if she were here.

Good thing she wasn't—not only because she knew him too damn well and never had a problem blabbing what she knew, but because he desperately wanted Kelly to himself.

Hell. *Desperately?*

He was bad off here, no doubt about it. A few minutes with Kelly again after a decade, and she was all he could think about. He was head over heels and falling fast.

All over again.

Was he ready for this?

As if he knew.

The host reappeared in the arch at the entrance, with Kelly right behind him.

The sight of her hit him like a punch to the gut. Her soft brown hair was chin-length now. The cut brought out her blue eyes and her mouth like a red bow. There had always been something…retro about her. He could picture her living way back in the Roaring Twenties, with a long string of pearls and a hip flask, dancing the Charleston 'til dawn. She wore a gray skirt that clung to her hips and flared at the hem. And a red blouse under a short jacket. She carried her coat over her arm.

She spotted him. Their glances held as she came toward him. He saw excitement in her eyes, an eagerness to match his own. That ripe bud of a mouth trembled on a smile. Was she nervous?

If she was, he understood. He was nervous, too.

He rose as the host pulled out her chair. They sat in unison. Then, when the host left, she got up and draped her coat behind her.

She asked for a glass of white wine and the waiter returned with it in no time.

And at last, they were left alone.

She smiled at him, the light from the candle glowing gold in her eyes. "So how did the book signing go?"

"I sold a lot of books and talked until my throat hurt. I think you could call it a success."

"Congratulations."

He shrugged. "I only hope the rest of the tour goes as well."

"And tomorrow you leave for…?"

"Seattle. From there, I move east. Minneapolis.

Chicago. New York. Then London, Paris, Stockholm and Berlin. And then back here to the States, to Dallas and L.A."

"Impressive."

"Well, the publicist I hired to set up the tour seems to think so. And I figure it can only help to get the word out."

"How long will all that take?"

"Three weeks. I'll be ready for a long rest by the time I get home."

"And home is…?"

"Mostly Los Angeles at this point. Though FirstJob.com is headquartered in Dallas, so I spend several weeks out of the year there."

"Wow," she said. "I can't get over all this. You really have come a long, long way."

He arched a brow. "From the Summer Breeze Mobile Home Park, you mean?"

She raised her wineglass. "Here's to you, Mitch." He touched his glass to hers and they drank.

"Now," he said, "about you…"

Something happened in her eyes. A certain… apprehensiveness. So. She had her secrets. He wanted to know them. Damned if he didn't want to know everything about her, to learn all that had happened to her in the decade since he'd lost her.

She asked, "What *about* me?"

"Tell me everything."

"Got ten years?"

"All right, all right. I guess I'll have to settle for the condensed version."

"Let's see. Where to begin? I'm the director of the Sacramento County Family Crisis Center."

"Sounds like an important job."

"Well, the service the center provides is important, that's for sure."

"Nonprofit, right?"

She laughed. He'd pay millions for that, just to listen to that laugh on a regular basis. Say, daily—morning, noon and at least twenty times a night. "Spoken like a true capitalist," she said.

"It wasn't a criticism."

"Well, good. And yes. We're nonprofit. We offer family counseling and a children's shelter for kids who need a place to go, temporarily, when there's a big problem." There was a proud gleam in her eyes.

"You believe in the work you do."

"I do."

"And you enjoy it."

"Yes." She ran a finger around the rim of her wineglass and slanted him a glance. "Mitch, I…" She seemed not to know how to finish.

He waited for her to go on. When she didn't, he asked, "How's your mom?"

She groaned and tipped her head back. "Oh, God. Now, there's a story…" She leaned toward him.

"You remember the famous Bravo Baby, kidnapped for a fortune in diamonds? The ransom was paid, but the baby was never returned to the parents."

"Of course, I remember." He reminded her, "You told me about him, back when we were together…."

"That's right. I did, didn't I? But ten years ago, nobody knew that the baby had lived, or who the kidnapper really was. I used to imagine I might be related to them, to that rich family named Bravo from Bel Air. I used to fantasize that I would go down there and knock on the door of their beautiful mansion. They'd know instantly that I was part of the family. They would want me to live with them, so I'd move into the mansion. I'd have a whole wing to myself…."

He couldn't get enough of just looking at her. Her skin had a tempting glow. He ached to reach across the table and brush her cheek with the side of his hand. Would her eyes go soft, welcoming his touch?

He asked, "You always wanted that, didn't you? A family of your own?"

"I did."

Ten years ago, he'd wanted to *be* her family. He'd wanted to be all she'd ever need. He'd *demanded* to be the center of her world. And because of that, he'd lost her.

He said, "It was five or six years ago, wasn't it, that they found out the Bravo Baby's kidnapper had been his own uncle? I remember reading about it."

It was a major story, all over the wire services and the talk shows. The notorious Blake Bravo, who had previously been declared dead in an apartment fire, had stolen his own brother's baby and lived for more than thirty years with no one knowing that he was very much alive the whole time. "He actually is dead now, right?"

"Yes. He's dead."

About then, Mitch realized where this story was headed. "Your own dad, the one you never met. His name was—"

"Blake. Yes. *The* Blake Bravo was my father. The Bravo Baby—all grown up now and living in Oklahoma City—is my cousin. And the famous Bravo Billionaire in his Bel Air mansion? He's my cousin, too. I was related to my fantasy family the whole time. Also, as it turns out, Tanner and I have half siblings all over the country. Beyond being a kidnapper and other scary things, my father was a polygamist. He married a lot of women.

"He would marry them and get them pregnant and then abandon them. If he did return, it was only long enough to father yet another baby. Oh. And that reminds me. Tanner and I have a sister, too—a full sister. My mother had a third child neither of us ever knew about. My sister is a couple of years younger than me. Her name is Hayley. She's married, with a new baby. Lives in Seattle."

"Slow down a minute. You're telling me that your mother had three kids and put them all in foster care…."

"And told each of us that us we were the only one. Yes."

Mitch had met Lia Bravo a couple of times back in the day. A thin, quiet woman with a faraway look in her eye. "She never seemed strong, your mother."

"She wasn't. She had no education to speak of and she had trouble keeping a job. She couldn't take care of us, and yet she would never agree to sign the papers so we could be adopted and maybe find new families for ourselves—and, as I said, she lied to us and never told us we had siblings. I don't know what drove her to do the things she did. I'll probably never know."

"What *drove* her? Past tense?"

"She died last May. That's how we found Hayley. We met her when we all just happened to show up in Mom's hospital room at the same time."

"Damn. That must have been quite a surprise."

"Oh, yeah. I look back and realize it would have been the same with Tanner and me, that we probably wouldn't have found each other until last year. We were lucky because Tanner vaguely remembered that there had been a baby when Mom put him in the system. Ten years ago, he had to practically blackmail her to get her to admit that yes, he did have a sister. One sister. She never did cop to Hayley's existence. So another decade went by before we found her."

He asked carefully, "You and Tanner are still close, then?"

"Very." Her smooth brow creased. "You don't still hate him, do you?"

Before he could answer, the waiter appeared. They took a few minutes to look at the menu and order.

Then they were alone again. And Kelly was watching him.

Time to face the music. From the moment he'd seen her the night before, standing there on the edge of that stage, he'd known he would find a way to be with her again—and that he would need to make amends.

He said, "I was way out of line. An idiot, ten years ago. Believe me, Kelly. I know that now. You heard me last night. It's a major point in my book and my lectures that ultimatums just don't work, but I made you choose between me and your newfound brother. All I can say is, I was eighteen and crazy in love with you and sure I would lose you—which, as it turned out, I did. Talk about a self-fulfilling prophecy. It was stupid. And self-defeating. And wrong."

Now her eyes were as soft as a summer sky. "So I left you—and then you lost your mom, too."

"Pneumonia. At least it was quick. Sometimes I

think she was relieved to go. She was never the same since we lost Deirdre—and my dad." Deirdre had been two years his junior. She'd died at the age of nine, hit by a drunk driver while she rode her new bike home from a friend's house down the street. His father couldn't stand the loss of his adored daughter and deserted them soon after. His mom had done her best, but they couldn't afford the house. She'd spent her remaining years in a cramped, single-wide trailer.

"Deirdre," Kelly softly whispered. Her eyes welled with sudden tears.

He did reach across the table then. "Hey." She let him take her hand. Damn, it felt good, just touching her. Her palm was soft and cool. "You would always cry, remember, whenever I talked about DeDe?"

She swallowed, nodded. "I…I knew you loved her very much. And nobody should die that young. It's just…so sad."

Even now, he could close his eyes and see her, his lost little sister. She would look up at him through those wide-set hazel eyes, trusting and proud to have him as her own big brother. "She was the greatest little kid. Nothing got her down, you know?"

Kelly glanced away. She swallowed again. "Mitch, I…"

"What? What's the matter? Whatever it is, just say it. I can take it, I promise you."

"Yes. I…well, I…"

The waiter arrived with their appetizers.

Kelly gently pulled her hand from his so the waiter could serve them. He asked if they wanted refills on their drinks. When they both passed, he left them.

"Now," Mitch said, "what is it you keep trying to tell me?"

"It's only that I…" she picked up her fork "…I want you to know that I did come back looking for you, a couple of months after I left…."

He shook his head. "Not a trace, huh?"

"No. The trailer had strangers living in it. They knew nothing about you. The guy in the park office told me about your mom and said he had no idea where you went. You'd left no forwarding address."

"I *had* no forwarding address. And we were renting the trailer. The weekly payment came due. I didn't have it. I realized I didn't want to be there, anyway. So I took what I could fit in my backpack and I hit the road."

"And you went…?"

"To Dallas. By way of L.A. and Las Vegas and Phoenix. I lived on the streets for about a year."

"Oh, I'm so sorry…."

"Why? It wasn't your fault. And living on the streets can be damn instructive—and you know what?"

"Hmm?"

"We've got this one evening. And then I'm on a plane tomorrow. Here we are again, after all these years. It's like magic. And I don't want to waste another minute of tonight talking about all the grim stuff we've been through since we were last together."

Another of those beautiful smiles trembled across her mouth. "Oh, Michael."

"Mitch," he corrected.

She sighed. "Mitch." She sent him a teasing look. "I like your attitude, Mitch."

"Well, I've been working on it for the past decade or so. It's good to know you see improvement."

"Oh, I do." She glowed at him. "I truly do. But as for the grim stuff, well, it's what made us who we are, right?"

"That's true."

She sipped the last of her wine. He had the feeling she was about to reveal something important, one of those secrets he couldn't wait for her to share with him, something about her life now that she found difficult to speak of. But then she only asked him more about himself.

"Your name. Why the change?"

He teased, "What? You don't like the name 'Mitch'?"

"I do like it. It just seems like a big step, I guess."

"People do change their names. It's more common than you might think."

"I'm not asking about 'people.' I want to know why *you* changed your name."

"I wanted to be...someone else. And now I am."

"But you *are* still Michael. Deep down. No matter how much you change."

He reached out. And so did she. Her fingers met his in the middle of the table, by the white magnolia blossom, in the candle's golden glow. Met. And held.

He said, "I'm not Michael. Not anymore. I'm someone different. Someone named Mitch. And believe me, I like myself as Mitch a whole lot better than I ever liked Michael."

"When did you change it?"

"When I was nineteen."

"A year after…"

"We broke up. Yes. By then I'd created my first video game and I was working on the second one. I had a little money, at last. I'd rented an apartment. It seemed like total luxury to me. To sleep in a bed, to finally stop wondering where the next meal was coming from."

"That must have been a great feeling."

"Clean sheets and food in my stomach. Oh, yeah."

She laughed again. "Actually, I meant how you came from nothing, and within a year you found success."

"Well, I still had a long way to go. But things were definitely looking up."

He'd still missed her like hell back then. It was an ache that never completely left him. But time had been kind and dulled the pain more year by year. He'd thought himself over her the past couple of years....

And then, last night, there she was, standing off to the side, her smile nervous and hopeful.

Since then, he couldn't stop thinking about her.

Again, she pulled her hand back. She picked up her fork and went to work on her asparagus salad. He ate some of his stuffed portobello mushroom appetizer. They were quiet for a few minutes. The food was good and the silence held promise it seemed to him.

Eventually, she asked, "Why Mitch Valentine?"

"Well, it starts with the same letters as my given name, so it was a change, which I wanted, but at the same time, it felt comfortable, you know? It felt... right. Familiar."

"But why Valentine?"

"Why not?"

"I don't know. It's not a name I can picture you choosing, I guess. It's a little too..." She couldn't find the right word.

He gave her some help. "Soft? Girly? Romantic? Imaginative? Kelly. I'm hurt. You don't think I'm imaginative...?"

She groaned. "Excuse me while I remove my foot from my mouth—and actually, I like it. It just surprises me you chose it, that's all."

"I actually did have a few reasons for making the choice. I'd already chosen Mitch some time before. As I said, I wanted a last name that started with a *V,* like Vakulic. And it was Valentine's Day when I went to see the lawyer about making the change. I thought, hell. Valentine. Vakulic. Same first *two* letters, just like Mitch and Michael. And I thought Valentine sounded like the name of somebody famous. I liked that. A lot."

She sat back in her chair. "So. That was nine years ago today…."

"That's right, now you mention it."

They shared a look. She broke the eye contact first. "Mitch," she said softly. Her mouth kept tempting him.

He wanted to kiss it. "I like it when you say my name."

There was urgency in those blue eyes. And something else. Something…what? Worried? Afraid? "Mitch, I…"

"What? Say it. Tell me."

She shook her head—and then she slid her napkin in beside her plate. "Be right back." And she got up and headed toward the arch that led to the ladies' room.

He watched her go, admiring the slim, softly curving shape of her, thinking that he was probably pushing too fast, promising himself he'd slow it down a little when she returned, smiling wryly as he realized there was no way he would keep that promise.

The ladies' room was blessedly empty. An orchid in a black pot graced the white marble sink counter. Beside the elegant flower a stack of neatly folded linen towels waited. So much nicer than ordinary paper ones.

Kelly braced her hands on the rim of the sink and leaned in toward the mirror. "You *will* tell him," she commanded in a whisper, glaring at her own image. "You will go back out there and you will tell him that he has a daughter and you will do it the minute your butt hits that chair."

She straightened. With slow deliberation, she smoothed her hair and then her skirt. She washed her hands and dried them on one of those beautiful cloth towels.

And then she drew her shoulders back and turned for the door.

At their table, the waiter was just setting down the main course. He slid over behind her and held her chair. She thanked him, he nodded and left them.

She spread her napkin on her lap again. *Tell him, tell him, tell him.* "This looks good…" She glanced up, into those amazing dark hazel eyes.

And she was lost. Finished. She just couldn't do it. He was there, across from her, after all these years. And somehow the boy she had loved had become the kind of man she dreamed about.

It was…a fantasy, this evening. *Her* fantasy. Just the two of them, by candlelight, sharing a lovely meal and good conversation.

Each glance was electric. And when he reached out and touched her hand…

Just a few more minutes. Just a little while longer.

She would tell him before they left the restaurant, before the night was over. But as soon as she did it, everything would change.

The fantasy would end. He would probably be angry. He would definitely be stunned. The hazy, soft magic between them would be blasted away.

Yes, she knew that every minute she kept the truth from him made her all the more culpable. Until last night, when she found him again, she was innocent of wrongdoing.

She'd tried to find him and failed, but she *had* tried. She'd had no thought, ever, of hiding the truth from him.

Now, though, this evening, as she sat here across from him, exchanged warm glances with him, told him of her life and urged him to tell her of his…

Now she was a cheater. A liar. Ultimately culpable. She knew it.

And still, she took her fantasy—stole it, really. She had her sweet, tender, romantic lie of an evening.

Because he drew her. Powerfully.

Because she wanted him.

Because she'd never felt like this with anyone, except Michael. And now, here he was, the Michael she'd lost all those years ago, reincarnated into an amazing man named Mitch Valentine.

They had coffee, after the entrée. And they shared a crème brûlée. The vanilla bean custard was warm, sweet silk in her mouth, and she looked across the table and thought of kissing him.

A long kiss. Slow and deep and lazy—and wet. A kiss that would be crème brûlée-sweet.

The look in those eyes of his told her he was thinking along similar lines.

By then, her evilness knew no bounds. She found herself imagining what it might be like to spend a whole night with him. They could go to his hotel, make love for hours on the white, white sheets of a huge hotel bed. She just knew it would be incredible.

And, of course, it was also impossible. First, she'd have to sneak off somewhere so Mitch wouldn't know what she was up to when she called Tanner.

She'd head for the restroom again, probably. By the marble sink with its linen towels and graceful orchid, she would auto-dial her brother. She would tell him that she'd decided to spend the rest of the night behaving inappropriately with the new, improved version of her high-school sweetheart. Would Tanner mind staying over 'til morning?

Tanner would ask the million-dollar question: Had she told Mitch yet that he was a dad?

She would have to say no, she hadn't. Not yet.

Oh, that would go over excellently. But just say, for argument's sake, that after Tanner finished telling her how badly she was handling this, he agreed to stay over and watch DeDe for the night....

Then what?

She'd have a whole night with Mitch. She'd have her fantasy come true.

Too bad about the next morning. By then, she would have run out of chances to put off the moment of truth. She would end up telling him about DeDe in the harsh light of the morning after, before he headed for the airport to board a plane.

How could he see that as anything but a gross and hideous betrayal?

Uh-uh. The evening was drawing to a close. They would not be going to his hotel together. The beautiful, sexy, romantic time was ending here. The fantasy was over before it ever had a chance to really begin. She did accept that.

And she needed to tell him about DeDe now, before they left the restaurant. She knew that. She did.

But still, she said nothing.

He paid the check. She thanked him. They rose.

He helped her with her coat and shrugged into his own. She felt his hand at the small of her back, a tiny gesture of care and consideration, one that echoed temptingly of possessiveness.

She wished he would keep his hand right there forever….

He guided her toward the door. She looked up at him and he smiled into her eyes and every atom in her body heated and bounced. A happy dance of the most elemental variety. She yearned for his kiss, for his hands on her bare flesh.

The host beamed and wished them a good evening. They nodded and thanked him. Mitch pushed the door open and they were out on the sidewalk in the cold night air.

It was quiet on the street, a weeknight in midtown. Another couple strolled by, arms wrapped around each other.

Mitch turned her to face him, at the same time as he pulled her a little closer to the building, into the shadows, out of the way of any more strolling pedestrians. He had both arms wrapped lightly around her and he gazed down at her and…

"Happy Valentine's Day," he said. His mouth descended.

She needed to tell him, before he kissed her.

But no. Once again, she surrendered to temptation. She lifted her mouth to welcome his kiss.

His kiss…

It was…everything she'd hoped for. It was her forbidden, lying fantasy fulfilled.

First, the touch—his mouth, her mouth. Nothing like it. She took his breath into her. It was as sweet as vanilla, rich as good coffee….

He deepened the contact. She sighed. Opened. Tasted him as he tasted her.

The same, she thought. *The thrill, the wonder, the delicious yearning that rode the fine edge between pleasure and pain. Still the same…*

His tongue swept in, teasing, caressing. He was the boy she had lived for and loved with all her yearning, hungry, lonely heart.

He was that boy. And more….

He framed her face, lifted his mouth from hers. She stifled a cry, to be losing such a kiss.

Oh, she didn't want this lovely intimacy to be over. She didn't want this magic to end.

His palms were warm against her cheeks, his fingers so gentle at her temples. "I used to think I would go after you," he told her. "That I would find you, that we could try again. But then, as time went by, I decided it was better, wiser, to let the past go…."

"Oh, Mitch. I know. I understand."

"But tonight…seeing you again, being with you again…"

"Yes. Exactly. Oh, I do know."

He took her shoulders. "Okay, this is crazy. But I don't want tonight to end. Do you think…is it possible that you could go with me, tomorrow?"

The question stunned her. She echoed, stupidly, "Go with you?"

"It's wild, I know. But wild doesn't have to equal impossible. All night, I've been thinking about how I might talk you into coming with me. I was thinking, what if I endowed that shelter of yours, gave them a big grant? Lots of money. You think it would be enough that they could do without you for a few weeks?"

"Oh, God."

He rubbed her shoulders, soothing her—and, oh, this was terrible. Why hadn't she told him an hour ago, *two* hours ago?

"Hey," he said. "Okay, maybe it's not possible. But well, I thought I'd at least give it a shot." His wry smile broke her heart.

Oh, to be able to simply say yes. To go with him, just pack a bag and take off, to follow this sudden, rekindled magic wherever it took them…

But who was she kidding? That couldn't happen. Even if she could somehow manage to take a few weeks off from the center with zero notice beforehand, there was DeDe to consider.

DeDe. His daughter.

The child she had yet to tell him about, though telling him had been the whole point of the evening.

Time was up. She knew it, accepted it. She'd stolen her little impossible fantasy, though she had no right to do it, though it only made this moment when the truth was upon her all the more painful.

He scanned her face, a frown forming between his brows. Something was very wrong and he was seeing that now. Still, he tried to play it light. "Okay, okay. I said it was a wild idea. Too wild, I guess. But a guy needs a fantasy, now and then."

"A…fantasy… Oh, Mitch." She took his big hands between her own. "I don't know how to do this. I've been trying all night, and failing miserably. I'm just so…attracted to you."

He looked at her sideways, with a teasing half grin. "And that's bad?"

"No. It's not. It's wonderful. Too wonderful. I didn't want it to end. I wish I could go with you, I swear, I do. I'm flattered and thrilled that you would ask me and I…" She squeezed her eyes shut. "Oh, God."

"What? What's gone wrong? I'm glad you still feel it for me. I feel it, too. I thought I'd made that clear. I thought we had something going here. Something good. Damn it, Kelly. Tell me what's wrong."

"I…"

"What?"

"When we broke up ten years ago?"

He nodded. "Yeah? What about it?"

"I was, um, pregnant."

He went absolutely still for a second or two—and then he moved, but only to pull his hands free of her hold. "What did you say?"

She prayed for the sidewalk to open under her feet, to just swallow her whole. "Oh, please, Mitch. Don't look at me like that."

He shook his head. "Pregnant? But you never said—"

"No, I didn't. Because I didn't know then. I didn't miss a period for two weeks after I left for Fresno with Tanner. And then it took me another few weeks to face the possibility, to admit what might be happening to me. When I finally took the home test, six weeks had gone by since we split up."

"All right." Now his voice was flat, devoid of expression. His eyes were shuttered—against her. "So. What happened then?"

"I tried to find you…."

"And you didn't. Got that. And then?"

"I…" She bumbled on, making a complete hash of it. "Seven months later, I had a baby."

He flinched as if she'd struck him. "No."

"Yes. I had a baby. *Your* baby. I had a little girl."

Chapter Four

"Oh, Mitch," she cried, moving toward him as he moved back.

He put up a hand to ward her off. And he spoke much too calmly, "You're joking, right?"

"No. No, of course not. I would never joke about something like this. I have a daughter. Your daughter. She's nine years old now. Her name is Deirdre. After your sister. We, um, we call her DeDe."

"DeDe," he repeated. "DeDe…"

"Mitch. Listen. Please don't be angry."

His gaze burned right through her. "What the hell kind of game are you playing?"

"No game. I swear to you. It's not a game."

"You sat there at that table with me, you told me all about yourself—except for one thing, the most important thing…."

"I'm sorry. I told you. It was…so great, to be with you again. I started enjoying myself. I…" She wrapped her arms tightly around herself against the night chill and tried to stand tall—and to keep her voice low and reasonable. "Look. I know I blew it. I should have told you right away, the minute I got to the table, I should have—"

"Try ten years ago. *That's* when you should have told me."

"How could I tell you then? I didn't know myself. And then, when I did come to find you, you were gone. You took off without leaving me any way to get in touch with you."

"You should have looked for me."

"I did look."

"I've got a pretty high profile. If you'd really wanted to find me, you would have."

"Mitch. You left the state. You lived on the streets. When you checked back in to the mainstream, you changed your damn name."

"You could have found me. That brother of yours, who finds people for a living, *he* could have found me."

"He tried. I swear to you. He's been trying all along. He—"

"Hold on." Those eyes of his had narrowed dangerously. "Money. That's it, isn't it? Money is what this is all about?"

"What?"

"Don't give me that sweet, bewildered look. I'm not buying. You want money. You've had a kid and you want to pass that kid off as mine, start collecting those fat child-support checks."

"That's ridiculous. And cruel."

"Hey. You should see it from where I'm standing."

A couple of men in suits and ties came out of the restaurant and headed for the side of the building and the valet parking stand. They were careful not to glance at Kelly and Mitch as they went by, but their presence brought it home to her that the two of them couldn't stand out here trading excuses and accusations all night.

She wrapped her arms tighter around herself and spoke in a tone just above a whisper. "Look. I know this has to be one hell of a shock to you. And I know that I screwed up. I handled this all wrong—if there even *is* a right way to handle telling a guy you had his baby nine years ago. But the fact remains, we had a child together. You have a daughter. You needed to know that. And now you do."

That seemed to settle him down. At least a little.

He turned from her, then turned back. He raised an arm and rubbed the back of his neck. "You're right. It's a shock."

"Yes. Of course. I understand."

"I don't know what to think. I'm going to need a little time to, uh, deal with this."

"Fine."

"I'll…be in touch. You can count on that."

"All right. However you want to handle…" She didn't finish. What was the point?

He was already walking away, his cell phone to his ear. "I'm ready," she thought she heard him say.

A long, black limo came rolling around the corner. It pulled to a stop. The driver got out, hustled around and opened the door. Mitch ducked inside.

Seconds later, the black car slid away from the curb and vanished into the night.

Tanner sat up and set down the remote. "So how'd he take it?"

Kelly tossed her coat and bag on an easy chair. "Not well."

Tanner stood. "Damn." He peered at her more closely. "Bad?"

"Real bad."

He swore. And then he edged around the coffee table and gathered her up in a hug. It felt good. Reassuring. To have her brother's strong arms around her.

When he let her go, he held her by the shoulders and met her eyes. "Give it time, huh? It'll work out."

"Oh, I don't know. He said some terrible things. He's really, really mad."

"What things?"

She didn't like the look in his dark eyes. "Oh, no." She shrugged free of his grip, shoved her purse out of the way and dropped to the easy chair. "Uh-uh."

Tanner played innocent. "What? I just asked what he said to you."

"You don't need to know."

"But—"

"Stop. You never liked him. I realize that. But he is DeDe's dad. Once he settles down a little, we're going to be dealing with him. I'm not giving you any more reason to be hostile toward him than you already are."

"I'm not hostile."

"I mean it. Stop."

Tanner loomed above her and glared at her for several painful seconds. Finally, he shrugged. "Fine. Don't tell me what a jerk he was tonight. I know the guy's an ass. No more proof is required."

Kelly rubbed her temples where a headache was beginning to pound. "He's not an ass. He's built himself an amazing life, starting from zip. He's smart and funny and warm. Yeah, he took the news about DeDe hard. But I put off telling him for much too long tonight. I kept promising myself I would do it—and then stalling. It was stupid. And wrong. I blew it, and that's a plain fact."

Tanner was scowling. "You were always too easy on him. And too hard on yourself."

With a sigh, she let her head fall back and closed her eyes. "Of course, you'd say that. You're my brother—and how have I been easy on him? I haven't seen him in ten years."

"You know what I mean—and you look beat."

"I am, as a matter of fact."

"Go to bed."

"I will. In a minute—and will you stop looming?"

He grumbled something.

She made herself lift her tired, aching head as he backed up and sat on the arm of the sofa. "Thanks for playing babysitter," she said.

"Hey. Isn't that what doting uncles do?"

"DeDe behave?"

He nodded. "She's a great kid. Hayley called."

"She okay?"

"She told me she's never been happier. I believe her. She sounded really good." Their sister and her new husband, Marcus, had separated after the holidays. But they were back together now and going strong.

"Since you are the most suspicious person in California," Kelly said, "if you tell me Hayley's happy, I know it's got to be true."

"A ringing damn endorsement if I ever heard one."

"You tell her where I went tonight?"

"Uh-uh. I left that to you. I told her you'd call her."

"Will do. In the morning."

Tanner glanced toward the floor-to-ceiling windows that looked out on the pool, which was covered this time of year. "I did a little research on Mitch, aka Michael."

"I knew you would."

"At least he's rich. I ordered his book on Amazon. It got reviewed in *Publisher's Weekly* and the *L.A. Times*. Good reviews."

"Don't look so surprised. Mitch is a very smart man."

"Coulda fooled me—I ordered you one, too."

"Thank you. You are an excellent big brother, you know that?"

"I do my best." He pushed himself upright again. "I'm outta here. Go to bed before you pass out in that chair."

"Hmm," she said, and leaned her head back again.

She heard the front door click shut as he left.

Kelly called Hayley the next day during her lunch break and told her what was going on.

"Imagine," her sister said, almost reverently. "Just like that. He's back in your life, after all these years."

Kelly chuckled. "Uh. Well. Not exactly. His last

words were *I'll be in touch.* Already, it's killing me, wondering what he'll do next, when—or where—he'll turn up. I'm telling you, I could get an ulcer, easy."

"I'm sure you won't have to wait long."

"For an ulcer?"

Hayley sighed, a patient sort of sound. "No, to see him again."

"Well, he's got a three-week, nonstop book tour happening as we speak. I'm not going to see him 'til after that's over, in any case."

"What about DeDe? Have you told her that her father's been found?"

"I've thought about it—all night long, instead of sleeping, as a matter of fact. But in the end, I decided to wait."

"For…?"

"To see what Mitch ends up doing about this. Last night he was pretty much in denial about the whole thing."

"Denial? Clarify. You mean, he didn't believe you'd had a baby—or he didn't believe that the baby was his?"

"Both, actually. It was a big shock for him and I did a bad job of telling him."

"How so?"

"God."

"You don't want to talk about it?"

"It's…just that I really blew it. It's embarrassing and I hate myself."

"So all right, you've proved it. You're human. Now, tell me."

"Well, there was this…instant attraction between us. I don't know what I expected, but not that. It was so long ago that I loved him. We were kids then. And he's so different now than he was then."

"Well, so are you."

"Yeah. Whatever. Anyway, we were both attracted. Powerfully. He remarked on it and so did I. I kept putting off telling him. I didn't want the evening to end, you know? Plus, I didn't really know how to say it, didn't know how go about it. It's such an impossible kind of thing to tell a man. But I managed it, finally. Not well, believe me. It came out sounding terrible, like some big lie I'd made up on the spur of the moment. He instantly accused me of tricking him, of stringing him along all evening without saying a word. It was bad."

"Yuck."

"Exactly."

"But now," Hayley said, "however hard it was for you to tell him, however badly it went, you've done it. The truth is out. He knows. Give him a little time to come to grips with the information, he'll be around."

"Oh, God. That's what I'm afraid of."

"I thought you *wanted* him to come around, to tell you what he plans to do about having a daughter."

"I do, I don't. I'm a human yo-yo and I hate it."

"Well, try and relax. You have at least three weeks before you have to deal with him."

"Three weeks. Right. At least, there's that."

A black limousine was snuggled up to the curb when Kelly got home at five-thirty that night. Mitch was waiting on her doorstep, hands in the pockets of his gorgeous winter coat. A thrill skittered through her at the sight of him and a bunch of fluttery creatures flapped their wings in her stomach.

He looked at her with a distressing mixture of dislike and impatience.

Nice. She had butterflies at the sight of him and the guy clearly despised her. How pitiful was that?

He muttered, "I wondered how long I'd have to wait out here," as she reached the concrete front porch.

"Excuse me. You're in my way," she said tightly, thinking, *So much for my three-week reprieve.*

He stepped aside. She unlocked the door and he followed her in. In the formal living room, which was through the arch a few feet from the door and faced the front of the house, she gestured to a wing chair.

He remained standing. "Where's the child?"

"She's at her modern dance class. She should be home by six-thirty."

"You pick her up?"

"No. We have a car pool. Today's not my day." *In more ways than one.* "What about Seattle?" He looked at her as if she'd just asked him a question in Swahili. She tried again and asked, "The book tour?"

"I've made arrangements."

"Arrangements for what?"

"I've cancelled the tour, indefinitely. Until this situation is resolved."

This situation? He made it sound like a crisis of epic proportions: a palace coup; a nuclear incident.

But then, well, for him—and for her and for DeDe—it *was* a big deal. A very big deal.

"Can you do that? Just cancel a big tour like that?"

"Well, since I've done it, I suppose the answer is yes." He looked around, at the sofa and matching patterned wing chairs, at the art she'd purchased with care and hung on the walls, at the long, padded bench beneath the new windows she'd had installed just last year. "Nice," he said, not surprised, exactly—but close.

"Thank you."

"Give me the address of the dance place. I'll pick up the child."

"DeDe. Her name is DeDe."

He said nothing. His mouth was a grim line and his eyes looked right through her.

There was no way she was letting this cold-eyed

stranger ride off in his limo to pick up her daughter. What if he scared DeDe? What if, God forbid, he tried to steal her away?

"We'll go together," she said, lifting her head high, pasting on a tight little smile.

"Suit yourself." He was already turning for the door.

"Wait!"

With clear reluctance, he faced her again. "What now?"

"We, um, don't have to go yet. It's only a few minutes' drive to the studio. Her lesson's just start- ing now…."

"Fine."

"Uh. Fine, what?"

"Don't those places usually have a seating area for the parents, so they can watch?"

"You want…to watch?" Why did that sound so awful?

His grim mouth grew grimmer. "Look. This isn't easy for me, okay? If I could see the kid ahead of time, before I have to figure out how to talk to her, that would be good."

"Good," she repeated.

"Good," he confirmed.

"She's a perfectly normal kid, I promise. Very… self-possessed for her age. You have nothing to be afraid of."

"How the hell do you know?" It was phrased as a question, but it came out sounding a whole lot like an accusation.

She tried not to flinch under the weight of his angry stare. "Tell you what. All right. You want to go, let's go."

During the short ride to the dance studio, Mitch refused to glance at Kelly even once. The backseat was plush and roomy, black leather and burled wood. She stayed on her side of the seat and he stayed on his.

He was good with that. More than good. She was trouble. Mitch knew that. He'd known it since she mangled his heart beyond all recognition ten years before.

She was trouble and yet she drew him. Still. He'd made the mistake last night of letting down his guard with her, of daring to imagine they might let the past go, try again together. Then, out of nowhere, she'd sprung the kid on him.

It was the last time she'd be messing him over. He would have a look at the kid, make arrangements for a paternity test. And if she was his, well, he was going to be a father to her. In more ways than with just his checkbook. The woman sitting next to him would damn well have to get used to his involvement in the kid's life.

Deirdre. He couldn't believe she'd had the nerve to give the kid his little sister's name—and yet Kelly choosing that name for her daughter seemed to make it more likely that the kid really was his. Why give some other guy's kid *his* sister's name?

Ten minutes after leaving Kelly's house, the driver let them off in front of Madame Arletty's International Dance Academy. He held the doors for them and then got back behind the wheel and rolled off down the street to wait until Mitch summoned him again.

The studio was a two-story brick building that took up half a block. Murals of figures in motion covered the walls on either side of the glass entry doors. A sign over the door advertised Ballet, Modern, Jazz, Tap, Ballroom and offered the phone number in three-foot-high numbers.

Beyond the glass doors, there was a reception area. An over made-up blonde gave Kelly a smile and a wave from behind a high desk.

Kelly led him down a hallway and up some stairs. Music seemed to seep out of the walls of the place: classical, jazz, a show tune accompanied by the sharp clicking of tap shoes on a wood floor.

At the end of a long hallway, Kelly pulled open a door. The music from in there was strange and without rhythm: wailing sounds and flute music punctuated by random drumbeats.

Kelly whispered, "This way."

As he'd expected, there was a row of plastic chairs that faced a large interior window. Two women in their late twenties or early thirties sat and watched what was happening beyond the glass. Kelly took a chair and Mitch sat beside her.

On the other side of the window, about twenty preteen girls in black tights moved to the weird music. Each kid seemed to be lost in her own little world, moving randomly, with no real rhythm or recognizable sequence. They swayed and waved their arms. They jumped and rolled. The teacher, a slim middle-aged woman with scraped-back hair and a narrow face, moved between the dancers, adjusting the position of one girl's arms, straightening the shoulders of another, nodding in approval one minute, shaking her head the next.

There were blond girls and brunettes, some chunky, some thin, all shapes and sizes and varying heights. There were white girls and black, Middle Eastern and Asian. At first, to Mitch, they were all a blur.

But after a minute or two, one with long, light brown hair caught his eye. She was turned away from the window so he couldn't have said what there was about her that drew him. Yeah, his sister had had brown hair. But so did several other girls in that crowded classroom. The one he noticed moved without much grace, but with great enthusiasm—

throwing her arms wide, fingers splayed, then rolling into herself.

Yes. There was something…

Kelly spoke in a whisper. "She's there…." And she pointed at the girl he'd already picked out.

And right then, staggering a little, all elbows and knobby knees, the girl turned and faced the window. He saw wide-set eyes, a round face, a happy, dimpled grin. And he knew that the paternity test wouldn't be necessary, after all.

The child was the exact image of the sister he had lost almost twenty years ago.

Chapter Five

The child—*his* child—perched on one of the plastic chairs at the observation window, finished tying her second shoe. She let both legs dangle. Mouth solemn, hazel eyes bright, she slanted Mitch a look.

"I know my mom told you my name is Deirdre, but she should have said to call me DeDe." She folded her hands in her lap, as if afraid he might expect a handshake.

"DeDe. Yes, I know."

"Mom says you're driving us home."

"That's right."

"She went to tell Mrs. Babcock I won't need a ride, after all."

"Yes. I know."

The child grabbed the quilted purple jacket she'd brought from her "cubby" and set it on the chair beside her while she put on her shoes. Beneath the jacket was a purple-and-lime-green backpack. While Mitch tried not to gape at her in awestruck wonder, DeDe put on the jacket and then pulled the purple backpack across her small shoulders. That accomplished, she folded those little hands in her lap again and swung her legs beneath the chair.

"Um. Are you sick or something?"

"No. Not at all. I'm fine. Just fine."

"You're sure acting funny."

"I am?"

"Well, you *are* staring."

"Oh. Well. Sorry." He made himself look away from her amazing face, resolutely aiming his gaze at the empty studio room on the other side of the glass.

Kelly reappeared at last. "Well. That's taken care of." She faked cheerfulness for all she was worth.

"Then are we going?" DeDe asked.

"Yes, we are." Kelly sent a resolutely bright look in his direction. "Ready?"

He nodded and rose.

DeDe slid down off the chair. "Ready." Mitch didn't miss the nervous glance she aimed at him.

He had to learn to relax around her. But every time he looked at her, he could hardly believe what he was seeing. His own kid, who had his dead sister's name and also happened to look just like her.

It was eerie. Strange. Way beyond weird. And soon he was going to have to tell her he was her dad.

Impossible. Capital *I*.

He'd created four businesses, still ran two of them. He owned a house in Turtle Creek, near Dallas and one in Malibu. He'd written a book about his own success and he had no trouble at all getting up in front of a packed auditorium and giving people advice as to how to make their lives work.

As a rule, he knew how to handle himself. He'd been called charismatic and brilliant, a powerhouse, a "motivator." With a great sense of humor.

So how was it that one round-faced, hazel-eyed kid had him tongue-tied and staring?

He shoved the question to the back of his mind and fell in step behind Kelly and the kid, remembering as they reached the top of the stairs that he needed to call for the car. He got out his cell and autodialed the driver.

"We're ready," he said when John picked up. His voice had DeDe glancing back, startled. Then she saw he was on the phone. Her look of relief almost made him smile. Evidently, she'd decided he was a very strange man, one who stared when he shouldn't and talked to himself.

The blonde with too much makeup waved as they went out.

The night was cold and clear. And the limo came sailing toward them.

DeDe beamed up at her mother, eyes as bright as stars. "Oh, Mom. A limo. You didn't say we would go in a limo."

"Only the best for us." She sent Mitch a smile that was all show and no substance, faking it for the kid. "Right, Mitch?"

"That's right."

DeDe rode between them. She chattered away through most of the short trip, admiring the TV screen suspended from the ceiling and fascinated by the GPS monitor built into the dashboard up in front. She discovered that her section of the seat had its own air conditioner/heating vent and she fiddled with that until Kelly told her to stop.

Then she begged for a 7-Up from the bar.

"Sure," Mitch gave her a nod. "Help yourself."

Kelly sent him a look that said, *Wrong answer.* "We'll be home in three minutes," she told the child. "Since Mitch says you can have it, okay. But don't open it until after dinner."

DeDe pulled a face. "But that's like an *hour* from now."

Kelly said nothing, only smiled sweetly and stared out the window.

"No fair," muttered DeDe. She clutched the can against her chest as if she feared her mother might snatch it away from her.

"And what do you say?" Kelly asked sweetly, still admiring the view from her side window.

Mitch wondered if she was talking to him—and if so, what the hell she meant.

Then DeDe looked up at him. "Thank you. For the 7-Up."

His heart did something kind of scary under his breastbone. It occurred to him that his life would never be the same. "Uh. You're welcome."

"Is he staying for dinner?" DeDe whispered.

Kelly dropped the spaghetti noodles into the boiling water. Mitch was in the family room, watching the news and calling people on his cell phone. Since he'd shown no indication he was leaving, Kelly told her daughter, "Yes. Go ahead and set a place for him."

"Is he like your boyfriend?" DeDe was frowning—and still speaking in whispers.

"He's…a friend. Why?"

"A friend from where?"

She and Mitch were going to have to talk. "I knew him when I was young."

"Young as me?"

"No, a little older. Set the table, please."

DeDe stayed where she was. "Is he sad or something?"

Kelly gave the pasta a stir and turned her full attention on her daughter. "Did he say he was sad?"

"No. Maybe he's lonely."

Kelly traced the line of DeDe's hair where it fell along her cheek, gently guiding the long, straight strands back over her shoulder. "Maybe you should ask him."

DeDe considered that suggestion as the television droned from the family room and Mitch, still on his cell phone, said something Kelly couldn't quite make out and Candy, stretched out on the floor by the kitchen table, lifted her hind leg and scratched her ear.

Finally, DeDe shrugged. "I think I'll just go ahead and set the table."

Kelly squeezed her shoulder. "Sounds like a plan."

They sat down to eat a few minutes later.

Evidently, Mitch had realized he needed to do more than stare at DeDe as if he couldn't quite believe she was real.

He asked her about her school and her teacher and her dancing lessons. DeDe, as a rule only too happy to talk about herself, gave one-word answers. She ate fast and asked to be excused in record time.

"I've got math homework," she claimed.

"Clear off your place, then," Kelly said.

DeDe had her plate scraped and in the dish-washer in thirty seconds flat. She headed for her room. Candy, tail wagging, limped along behind.

Kelly looked across at a glum-faced Mitch. There was the sound of DeDe's bedroom door closing down the hall. "More wine?"

"She hates me."

She handed him the bottle and watched him refill his glass. "Give her time."

"How long?"

"Sorry. Believe it or not, I don't have all the answers."

He glowered. "And now I get attitude from you. Wonderful." He knocked back a big slug of wine.

She reminded herself that this was a difficult situation and there was nothing to be gained by the two of them getting into an argument. She spoke softly. "Look at it from DeDe's point of view. She's nine. A stranger, a grown man, shows up at her dance lesson. He seems upset about something. And he also seems very interested in her, for no reason she can understand."

He glowered some more. "What are you getting at?"

"Even kids can be suspicious. She doesn't know where you fit in."

"She asked you about me?"

"Yes. She wanted to know if you were my boyfriend. I told her you were a friend of mine—though we both know you're not and I'm sure she knows it, too."

He set down his wine and sneered, "I should be nicer to you, is that what you're saying?"

Again, she reminded herself that she wasn't going to fight with him, no matter how much he provoked her. "If you're asking for my opinion, what you should do is tell her that you're her father. You should tell her right away."

"I didn't ask for your opinion."

"Well, too bad. You got it anyway." Resolutely, she twirled spaghetti onto her fork and poked it into her mouth. He watched her as she chewed. She swallowed, hard. "What? Have I got spaghetti sauce on my chin or something?"

He turned his wineglass by the stem. "I think it's a bad idea to spring something like that on her when she doesn't even know me."

She thought that was pure crap, though she showed the self-restraint not to say it in so many words. "However, it's a *good* idea for her to know where you fit into her life."

"Not yet." He lifted his glass again, sipped, savored. And then said offhandedly, "I was planning to arrange for a paternity test."

"Look. Whatever you feel you have to do. Up to a point, anyway."

"What point is that?"

"You'll know if you go too far with me, Mitch. Trust me on that." It gave her bleak pleasure to discover she sounded a lot more sure of herself than she felt.

He regarded her darkly for several seconds. "As I was about to say, the paternity test won't be necessary. I know she's mine."

Mine. Kelly didn't like the way he said that. *Mine,* as in *nobody else's, not even yours…*

Was he telling her she was in for a custody battle? God help her. *Don't borrow trouble, take it one step at time.*

As to the question of a paternity test, Kelly had been pretty confident he wouldn't ask for one—not after he'd set eyes on DeDe. Years ago, he'd shown her the family album, with pages and pages of pictures of his sister. There was no mistaking the resemblance between DeDe and her namesake.

She said, "The test is your choice. I can see how it would matter to you, to know for sure."

"I do know for sure."

"Well, all right then. More spaghetti?"

"No, thanks."

She rose and carried her plate and the salad bowl to the sink. She was scraping the plate when she felt him behind her. She opened the dishwasher and put the plate in, turning to him as she straightened.

He was much too close. He had his empty plate in one hand, the bread basket in the other.

"Set the basket on the counter," she said as she took the plate from him.

Before she could turn to the sink again, he caught her arm. A hot little thrill ricocheted through her. She hated that, the way he excited her.

He had no damn right to turn her on. He was hostile and hateful and she wanted, very badly, to simply despise him. Or better yet, to feel nothing at all.

"This is a nice house." He said it with a cruel kind of tenderness that sent a burning shiver running right under the surface of her skin.

"Your point being?"

"Nice. And roomy."

She was getting a very bad feeling that she knew where he was going with this. "I was lucky. I got it at auction for half what it was worth when I bought it. I never could have afforded it, otherwise."

"When was that?"

"Four years ago."

"I notice there's even a pool."

"Yeah. It needed work. Truthfully, the whole house needed a fat infusion of cash and a lot of TLC when we moved in. But little by little, I've been pulling it together."

"Good for you."

"Tanner helps."

"Oh, I'll bet."

"Would you please let go of my arm?"

He released her. But he didn't step back. "How many bedrooms?"

"Look. You want a tour?"

"Just an answer will do."

"Four bedrooms. DeDe's. Mine. I use the one in the front hall as an office."

"And then there's the guestroom." He smiled. Slowly.

He had her boxed between the sink, the *L* of counter on one side and the open dishwasher on the other. She backed up until she touched the sink rim. Nowhere else to go. "Okay. I know what you're getting at. And I just have to tell you I think it's a really, really bad idea."

"That I want to be near my daughter is a bad idea?"

"That's not what I meant."

"Oh, no?"

"Why not go back to your luxury hotel? Enjoy room service and maids scurrying around cleaning up after you. DeDe's only here in the morning and evening, anyway. Even on weekends, she's got a million things going on. Staying here won't mean you'll see her any more often than you would otherwise. And of course, you can visit whenever you want."

"I don't want to *visit*." He said the word as if it

disgusted him. "I'm thinking immersion is the way to go. I want her to become accustomed to having me around. It should happen on her turf, so I become a part of her life before I tell her who I am."

"Why?"

"So it's not a shock to her."

"There's no way of knowing how she'll react when she finds out. She could feel tricked if you wait too long to tell her."

"Tricked. Right. I know how that feels."

"I didn't trick you, Mitch. Yes, I took too long to tell you that you have a daughter. And you *felt* tricked. Just like DeDe might feel tricked if you get to know her under false pretenses."

He was silent for a moment. She almost dared to hope she'd gotten through to him. But then he said, "No. I don't want to tell her yet."

Lord, grant me patience. "I think you're wrong."

"Duly noted."

"And how long of an *immersion* are we talking about here?"

"So. You agree." The light of triumph flared in his eyes. "I'll be staying in the guest room."

"No, I don't agree. But if you insist, well, I feel it's important that you have your chance to get to know Deirdre, however you want to handle doing that."

"Good then." He took out his cell phone and auto-dialed a number, while he kept her trapped against the sink. "John. I'll be staying here. Get my bags from the concierge at the hotel, will you? Great." He flipped the phone shut and put it away. "He should be back within an hour."

"When will you tell her?"

"I don't know. When I feel the time is right."

"Could I just have a ballpark figure, you think? Two days? Three?"

"Maybe longer. How can I say? Not until she's comfortable around me, not until I think she's ready to hear it. As of now, I have no idea how long that's going to take."

Chapter Six

"If he has a limo, why doesn't he have a house to live in?" In the light of the ballerina lamp by her bed, DeDe was looking doubtful.

Kelly smoothed the covers and kissed her cheek. Her daughter's breath smelled of cinnamon toothpaste and her skin was still pink from her bath. "He has a house—two, as a matter of fact. One in Texas and one by the beach in Los Angeles."

DeDe made a disapproving sound. "But if he has two houses, why does he have to stay here?"

"Because he doesn't have a house in Sacramento.

And he's…my friend. So of course I would invite him to stay at our house."

"Mom." DeDe's voice was very serious and her frown was severe. "Are you going to marry that guy?"

Kelly had to hold back a sudden burst of shocked laughter. "Whatever gave you that idea?"

"Well. Are you?"

"No. Of course not."

"Good. Because he doesn't even seem to like you very much. And I don't want a stepfather, anyway. Devon Marie and Lindsay have stepfathers." The two girls were DeDe's school friends. "A stepfather has to like you and you have to like them. But maybe sometimes you really don't like them, whether you're s'posed to or not—but then there's Alicia." Alicia was in a couple of DeDe's dance classes, and her mom was part of their car pool. "Alicia says *her* stepdad is more like a dad to her than her *real* dad."

"Well, see. There you have it. Each situation is different and a stepfather can be a very good thing."

"So you maybe might marry him, then? You can tell me. It's probably better if I start getting used to it."

"Honey, no. Mitch will never be your stepfather." Okay, she felt a twinge of guilt when she said that, given the way she failed to add, *because he's already your father.*

But she'd agreed to let Mitch tell his daughter

who he was in his own way. It seemed a promise she was duty-bound to keep, the least she could do for him when he'd missed the first nine years of his little girl's life.

She added, "He's just a friend-friend, not a boyfriend. Honestly."

DeDe untangled a small hand from her nest of blankets and grasped Kelly's shoulder. She looked at her mother levelly. "If you like him and he's your friend, well, I guess we have to let him stay here."

"I'm so pleased you see it that way."

DeDe brightened. "Maybe we can teach him how to not be so lonely and sad."

"Well, I don't really know if that's something you can teach someone. Plus, I'm not sure Mitch is lonely and sad. But still, he's a guest in our house and we want him to be comfortable here."

DeDe tucked her hand back under the blankets. "Mom. Don't worry. I'll be nice to him."

"I know you will." Kelly bent close and kissed her daughter's cheek one more time. "'Night."

"'Night."

Kelly turned off the ballerina light and closed the door behind her.

And jumped at the sight of Mitch, lurking in the doorway of the guestroom down the hall, wearing sweatpants and a T-shirt. He tipped his head toward the room behind him.

She longed to simply turn and head the other way. What more could they possibly have to say to each other tonight?

Nothing good, she would bet.

But in the interest of getting along, she went where he wanted her. He stepped aside so she could enter and shut the door once she was inside, closing them both in the room together.

Kelly edged away from him, toward the door to the bathroom. He was in the process of unpacking. A suitcase was spread wide on the bed. The closet door stood open and she could see a pair of black garment bags hanging in there. In the bathroom, a leather shaving kit waited on the counter by the sink.

She said, unnecessarily, "The three top bureau drawers are empty. Feel free to use them."

"Thanks. I will." He folded those amazingly muscular arms across his big chest and seethed at her. Really, he'd been seething steadily since last night when she'd rocked his world with the news that he was a dad. Where *was* the charming, reasonable man she'd met at Valley U just forty-eight hours ago? Would he ever return?

She felt trapped and she wanted out of there. "Okay, then." She started toward him, playing it confident and brisk, willing him to step aside so she could go. "If you've got everything you need, I'll just…"

He remained, arms folded, directly in her path. "What did you tell her about my staying here?"

Enough. She mirrored his pose. "That's twice tonight you've boxed me in. First at the sink, and now this. I don't like it. Don't do it again."

"I don't trust you."

"No kidding. I'm leaving this room. Get out of my way."

"Listen—"

"No." She jabbed an index finger at him. "*You* listen. I understand that you're furious at me. That you feel cheated. And wronged. I even sympathize. I can't begin to imagine what you must be going through, learning you have a child, dealing with the reality of her, having to figure out how to be a father to her, how to tell her who you are, how to…change your life to fit her into it. I get it, okay? I honestly do. And whether you believe me or not, I want to help you any way I can. As much as it's going to change my life and DeDe's life, it's important that you're here, that she gets her father and you get your daughter."

"Well. At least you—"

"*But,*" she said strongly, and then waited to make sure she had his attention. "I am not going to help you if you keep pushing me around. This isn't easy for me, either. And damn it, you're going to have to work *with* me, or you will be leaving my house."

Had she reached him, had she cracked the hard shell he seemed to have locked around his heart? Not. But he did at least relax his hard stance a little.

Instead of glaring daggers at her, he looked at a point over her left shoulder. "I'm sorry," he said, in a tone a little too noble to be convincing. "You're right. This is your house and I…" he hesitated "…I've been pushing you too hard. I'll back off."

"Well. That's something."

"I shut the door so DeDe wouldn't hear us, not to intimidate you." He moved away from the door. "Go if you want. But I was hoping…" He let the words trail off.

And she was such a sucker. She *had* to ask, "Hoping what?"

"That you would tell me what she said about my staying here." A hank of dark brown hair fell over his forehead. He looked so handsome, so…manly. She longed to step up close to him, to smooth that unruly hair back into place.

Of course, she did no such thing.

And truly, he didn't have a clue about how to get to know his daughter. "Mitch, you act like she's some…other species, or something. Or someone from some strange foreign land with customs you don't understand. She's just a little girl."

"I'm not around kids much."

"Clearly." She laughed softly, to try and lighten

the mood a little. "And if you really want to know what she said, she asked why, if you had a limo, you didn't have a house."

His lips twitched with the beginnings of a smile—and then he picked up on the deeper implication of DeDe's remark. The hint of good humor vanished. "You mean she doesn't want me here."

Kelly backed up enough to perch on the straight chair in the corner, by the nightstand. "Yes, DeDe's mistrustful of you. And why shouldn't she be? You're not being honest with her and she senses that you're not. She knows something's going on here, she just doesn't know what."

He had his arms folded over his chest again. "I'm not telling her until she knows me better and that's that."

She put up both hands. "Okay, okay. You're doing it your way. Got that message. Loud and clear." She stood. "Anything else?"

"Tomorrow. What's DeDe's schedule?"

"School until four. Then her ballet lesson from four-thirty to five-thirty."

"I'll drive her. To school and to the lesson."

"Do you mind if I make one tiny suggestion?"

His answer was a half shrug.

She said, "Let her ride the bus to school with her friends, the way she always does. Don't be all over her. Give her a little space."

"What about the lesson?"

"See, you want to drive her places like her new-found dad would do, but you don't want to tell her that you *are* her dad. That's not going to cause anything but trouble."

"How about if I offer to drive her *and* her friends to the lesson? If she says no, so be it."

Kelly shook her head. "Great. Setting it up so the child makes the choices…"

"Come on, damn it. I'm trying to get to know her."

She reminded herself that *he* had to have a little space, too. He had to make his own mistakes the way most new parents do. "Okay. Ask her in the morning. Fine with me."

In her own bathroom, Kelly washed her face and brushed her teeth. She stretched out on the bed and reached for the novel she'd been reading—and then realized she'd better tell Tanner what was going on at her house.

She called his cell, got his service and left a message.

He returned the call ten minutes later, as she was lying on her back with her fingers laced behind her head, staring through the darkness at nothing in particular. She told him that Mitch was staying in the guest room indefinitely. "He says he wants to get to know her before he tells her he's her father."

"Stupid," said Tanner.

"Just thought you ought to be forewarned. Still want to come to dinner Sunday night?"

"You think maybe he'll be gone by then?"

"In three days? Not likely. But it *could* happen."

"Well. I can hope...."

"You're going to have to make your peace with him, you know?"

"Don't remind me. And what happens next?"

"Next?"

"Once he finally breaks the big news to DeDe?"

Dread settled over her. "We haven't gotten that far yet." Mitch had said that he lived in L.A. most of the time. And also in Dallas. Would he want DeDe with him, at least part of the time?

Probably. If they were fortunate, he'd take certain weekends and holidays and a few weeks in the summer, so that DeDe could continue at the school she knew, with the friends she'd had just about all her short life.

If they were fortunate...

"You still there?" asked Tanner.

"Right here."

"Thought I'd lost you, you were so quiet."

"Yeah, well...guess I was borrowing trouble there for a minute."

"Don't. I'll be there Sunday. And if Mr. Personality is still hanging around, I promise to be on my best behavior."

"Couldn't ask for more."

"Sure you could." He said good-night and they hung up.

She lay there awake in the dark for another hour or so, borrowing trouble as she kept telling herself she wouldn't. Worrying about the man in the guest-room and the thousand and one ways he was going to change all their lives.

Mitch tried not to stare at his daughter as she shoveled cold cereal into her mouth. There was a drop of milk on her chin and her tan-colored hair had been brushed smooth and fell, as straight as a silk curtain, down her small back. She wore a fluffy green sweater and a short denim skirt with tights and black shoes with buckles. She picked up her napkin and rubbed the milk off her chin.

He sipped his coffee, tried to look casual. "Say, DeDe…"

She swung those wide-set eyes his way and ate another spoonful of cereal.

"Your mom tells me you've got a ballet lesson after school."

"Mmm-hmm." More cereal was scooped and devoured.

He felt ridiculously nervous, though he already knew what he'd do if she said no: nothing. "How about if I pick up you and your friends and take you to the dance studio?"

DeDe frowned. "And then take us home?"

"That's right."

"Mrs. Lu is s'posed to drive us today...."

He pictured himself calling the other kid's mother. What would he say? *I'm Deirdre's father but she doesn't know it yet.* Or *I'm a family friend of the Bravos and I'd like to drive the kids to their dance lesson today....*

Now, that would go over big. What would a mother think of a grown man who couldn't wait to drive a bunch of little girls around?

Across the table, Kelly was watching.

Being a secret father had all kinds of drawbacks. And did Kelly's eyes say *I told you so,* or was that only his frustration talking?

"Tell you what," he said to DeDe. "Maybe Kelly and I will just show up and watch you while you have your lesson."

DeDe frowned at her mother.

Kelly said, "Mitch. I work until five. It's doubtful I could get there in time to see much of the lesson."

DeDe spoke up then. "But you could come by yourself, Mitch. I mean, if you want to...."

Triumph! A major breakthrough. His daughter had actually invited him to come watch her dance lesson. He was the happiest man on the whole damn planet.

But he remembered what Kelly had told him, about giving the kid space. He sipped coffee and played it offhand. "I'll be there."

DeDe nodded. "Okay."

Once she'd left for school, Kelly gave him a key to the house. "Because I suppose you're going to need some way to get in and out when I'm not here." She set it on her side of the table and gave it a push.

He caught it before it slid off on his side. "Thanks."

"You need to tell her."

Actually, he *had* been thinking about that. A lot. And not just during breakfast, but all last night, as well. "I know."

She looked at him, almost smiling. He thought about how much he liked the bow shape of her mouth, about how he still wanted to kiss her, even though that would be a bad idea. He didn't trust her. *Couldn't* trust her—not any more than he had to, given that they shared a daughter. No matter how she tried to deny it, she'd kept his child from him. She might claim she'd had that brother of hers looking for him, but he didn't buy it. He never would.

She said, "You've reconsidered. About telling her."

"Yeah. I think you have a point. It's like lying

to her, not to tell her who I am. So I'm going to do it."

"When?"

"Tonight."

DeDe's ballet lesson was at the same dance studio, in a room on the first floor. Like the room upstairs it had an observation area for the parents.

All but two of the chairs were taken. Mitch was the only male in sight—on either side of the observation window. He took one of the free seats.

The class hadn't formally started yet. The students were warming up on their own. DeDe spotted him and waved as the instructor, a regal woman with short red hair and excellent posture, clapped her hands for attention.

There was a half hour of what looked to Mitch like warm-ups at the bar, the feet moved into various positions, lots of leg-lifting and—what did they call those—pliés?

Next, they did runs and twirls out on the floor. DeDe was pretty bad at all of it. Hard truth, the kid was a terrible dancer. Even Mitch, who knew less about ballet than he did about nuclear physics, could tell that.

But he didn't care how uncoordinated she was. He thought she was the cutest damn thing he'd ever seen. There was something to be said for giving it your all. And DeDe did that. The kid had heart. She would never be a professional dancer, but whatever she ended up choosing to do with her life, Mitch had no doubt she'd give it a hundred and ten percent.

She disappeared once the class was over and he figured she'd already gone off with her friends. He sat there for a few minutes, staring into the empty classroom, feeling kind of bereft that she was gone—and knowing that was patently absurd, since he'd see her again at the house soon enough.

"Hey, Mitch." He looked over and there she was, a few feet away, that purple jacket across her arm and her backpack hooked on one shoulder. "Since you're here and everything, I told Mrs. Lu I'd go ahead and get a ride with you."

Happiness, like sunshine, seemed to light up the world. "Uh. Great. I'd be glad to drive you."

"She had to call Mom—Mrs. Lu did. Even though I told her it was okay if I rode with you."

"Always good to play it safe." He stated the obvious and couldn't believe how lame he sounded.

"I already changed into my street shoes." She looked down at her feet and then back up at him.

"Ready to go, then?"

She dropped her pack, pulled on her jacket and then put the pack back on. "Yep. You should call."

"Call?"

She grinned. "For the limo."

"May I please have a 7-Up?" she asked the moment they got in the long, black car.

"Yes. But save it 'til after dinner."

She groaned in protest, but more for show than anything else. Then she opened the bar, took out the can and pushed the bar shut again. "There." She sat back into the tufted leather seat again. "I really like the way that works. I mean, if you didn't know where to push, you might not even know all those drinks were in there."

"No, you might not."

She held the soda on her knees, in both hands. "I like this limousine."

He'd been thinking he'd have to go out and rent a car, instead of keeping the limo on call all the time. But for now, let her enjoy the ride. "I like it, too," he said.

She leaned his way and pitched her voice low. "The man who drives is very quiet. Does he have a name?"

"John."

"Should we thank him—for driving us?"

Mitch pushed the button that rolled down the privacy screen. "John?"

"Mr. Valentine?"

"DeDe here would like to thank you."

DeDe spoke right up. "John, you're a good driver. Thanks."

"My pleasure, DeDe," said John.

Mitch rolled the screen back up and DeDe giggled.

There was a silence. He turned to look at the child at the other end of the seat and saw she was watching him, eyes suddenly somber, wide mouth so serious.

Had he done something, *said* something to upset her? A moment ago, she'd seemed fine. "DeDe? What's wrong?"

"I have a question." Her glance slid away. She clutched her 7-Up as if it were a lifeline.

"Go ahead. Ask me."

She gulped. "This is really hard…."

"Come on. It's okay. Don't be afraid."

Those hazel eyes met his again. "Well. Last night, after Mom tucked me in?"

"Yeah?"

"I got up and I got out my baby album—you know, with pictures and stuff from when I was born?"

"Yeah?" he said again, though the saliva had dried up in his mouth and his heart was knocking loud and hard inside his chest.

"There's two pictures of my dad in there. One of them, you can see his face real clear."

"His…face?"

"He was a lot skinnier than you. And not so old as you, you know?"

"Uh. Yeah. I know."

"And his name was Michael. Michael Vakulic."

"Yeah…"

"But, um, even though he was skinny and he had a different name, well, he kind of looks like you."

Now he was the one gulping—and all he could say was, "Ah. Yeah. Well, I…"

And then she asked him the question, the amazing, impossible question.

"Mitch, are you my dad?"

Chapter Seven

"Are you going to throw up?" The child—his daughter—looked at him with nervous concern.

Haltingly, he reassured her. "I'm… No. I'm not. Seriously. I'm okay."

She wasn't buying. "You don't look so good."

"You…surprised me, that's all."

A silence. DeDe clutched her soda can and waited. Mitch had a million things to say to her, but somehow, he just sat there, amazed and shaken. All last night and all day today, his mind had been filled with one big question: How would he tell her who he really was to her?

And now…the question was answered. There was no need to tell her. She'd figured it out for herself.

The kid was astonishing—and about a thousand miles ahead of him.

Finally, she asked in that tiny, shy voice, "Well. *Are* you?"

He knew there was something meaningful and ideal he could say. *Should* say. If only he wasn't so damn blown away. The seconds ticked by.

In the end, he had to settle for the plain, unvarnished truth. "Yes. I am. I am your father."

He heard her sigh. And then she smiled. And then she relaxed her grip on her can of 7-Up. "That was hard."

"No kidding."

Kelly got home at five-thirty. She changed into jeans and a sweater, slipped on a pair of flats and then headed for the kitchen to check the slow-cooker chicken and cut up a salad.

The chicken was ready. She turned the dial on the cooker to warm and resisted the urge to just go ahead and set the table. That was DeDe's job and she should be home any minute—with Mitch, according to the phone call she'd received from Eve Lu.

Mitch. *Tonight,* he had said. He would tell DeDe tonight.

Kelly stood at the sink and stared at the window

that looked out on the backyard. Now, after night-fall, she saw only her shadowed reflection in the darkened glass. Their lives would be changing.

Changing in a big way. Was she ready for the change? Not in the least.

But it was coming, anyway.

Behind her, she heard Candy come in through the laundry room and the dog door there that led out to the side yard. Her claws tapped the floor as she limped over to drink from her water bowl. The lapping, splashing noises started. Kelly smiled at the sloppy sounds and reminded herself that change was inevitable. And she'd known all along anyway, that when they found Michael, *if* they found him, their lives would never be the same.

Too bad there was such an enormous divide between knowing a thing and then actually having to live it.

She heard the front door open. "Mom!"

Kelly put on a smile and turned. DeDe came bouncing into the kitchen, clutching a can of 7-Up, Mitch close behind her. "Mitch brought me in the limo, after all."

"I hope you had a great ride."

"We did." DeDe glanced back at Mitch, who nodded as if affirming some past agreement. Then she plunked the can down on the table and came flying right at Kelly. "Oh, we did. We did!" She wrapped her arms hard around Kelly's waist and pressed her face against her sweater.

"Whoa…" Kelly laughed and hugged her in return.

And then her daughter looked up at her through shining eyes. "I know he's my dad, Mom. I asked him and he told me it's true."

"Well," said Kelly, holding on tight, smoothing her daughter's brown hair. "That's good. That's very, very good…" She looked up and met the watchful gaze of the man across the room.

Change. Inevitable. And coming at them fast.

That night, Mitch did tucking-in duty. Kelly waited in his room for him. The minutes dragged by. He was in there a long time.

She told herself a father/daughter bedtime talk was a good thing. He and DeDe had a lot of catching up to do.

At last, he appeared in the doorway. He looked surprised to see her there.

She'd taken the straight chair in the corner, but found she couldn't sit still. She rose. "I… Well, we do need to talk. Behind a shut door, I think."

He frowned. "Why shut the door?"

God save me from a man who knows nothing about kids. And what? Did he think she would try to take advantage of him or something?

Patiently, she explained, "DeDe is nine. Yes, she

knows better than to listen in on adult conversations. But that doesn't mean she won't—especially if she thinks what the adults are saying might be important to her."

He just stood there, looking disdainful—not to mention, much too handsome. What was it about him? The air around him seemed to crackle with pure male energy. It was beyond annoying. The guy had made it crystal clear he despised her. And yet, she kept obsessing over how manly he was, kept thinking that if he *did* make a move on her, she'd have a very hard time remembering all the reasons she intended to say no.

She suggested, "If you'd be more comfortable, we could go in my office."

Another long, aloof look. And then he stepped into the room and shut the door. "All right. Talk." Big arms folded. Jaw set.

She sat down again. *Talk.* He sounded like one of the detectives on *Law & Order.* What did that make her? The perp?

Really, dealing with him was no fun at all. But she owed it to their daughter to keep on trying. "I'm so glad that Deirdre finally knows who you are." She paused, hoping he'd agree. That would start them off on a common footing.

But he said nothing, just stood there, arms

crossed, muscles hard and bulging under his black cashmere sweater.

She soldiered on. "And, well, now that she does know, we need to discuss how we're going to work out where she'll be staying and when. I was thinking—"

"No," he said, and went on glowering.

She cleared her throat. "Excuse me. You don't even know what I was going to say."

"I know what you *did* say."

She tried to follow. "You mean, that we need to discuss—"

"Exactly."

"Well, Mitch. We do need to discuss custody, as difficult as that discussion might be—for me, and for you, too, I'm sure."

"Not now, we don't."

"Um. Because?"

"DeDe and I have talked about it."

Kelly took a minute. She breathed in slowly through her nose, let the breath out with care. She crossed her legs, smoothed her jeans, though they hardly needed smoothing. And then, when she felt she could speak without raising her voice, she said, "You discussed DeDe's custody arrangements with her—before you talked to me about it?"

"That's right." He actually looked on the verge of sheepish, though he maintained his wide-legged, commanding stance. "It…came up just now, while I was telling her good-night."

"Came up? All by itself?"

"No. I brought it up, if you need specifics."

"I do. I need specifics."

"I don't like your attitude, Kelly."

"Too bad. So. You brought up her coming to live with you part of the time."

"That's right."

"And you said…?"

"Just that. I said that now I'd found her, I would want her with me half the time, however we ended up working that out."

Kelly's stomach knotted. "Half the time? But she's in school nine months out of the year…"

"I realize that. Remember, though, there are weekends and holidays to consider, as well. And since I can afford to fly her wherever I happen to be when she's free, it seemed a reasonable way to handle the situation. When she's in school, she would be here, with you—and the rest of the time, she'd be mine."

"Yours…"

"What? You're offended that I call her mine?"

The knot in her stomach loosened. Now, she felt weak. Hollowed out, somehow. DeDe, living elsewhere half the year…

How would she bear it? Life would seem so empty.

But wait a minute.

Mitch had a right to a life with his daughter. And Kelly was just going to have to learn to share. Eventually. When DeDe was ready. When Kelly was certain Mitch was up to the job.

"No," she told him. "I'm not offended. DeDe *is* yours. She's your daughter and you have every right to expect to have her with you That's what we need to talk about. I think we need to take it slow."

He grunted. "Spoken like the woman kept her from me for nearly a decade."

Calm, she thought. *Easy...* "I did not keep her from you. I couldn't find you."

"Look. Let's not get in to that right now."

She gaped. "Who brought it up?"

He looked totally put-upon. "I don't want to fight with you, Kelly."

She took more deep breaths and kept her mouth shut.

Finally, he muttered, "The whole custody issue is completely moot for the time being, anyway."

Kelly blinked. "Okay. Not following."

"DeDe said she doesn't want to live anywhere but here."

Kelly sat up straighter. Yes, she would *love* to have her daughter all to herself for the next nine years or so. She would adore not ever needing to have this conversation. But...

"DeDe's a child," she said.

His look disdained and dismissed her simultaneously. "Were you under the impression that I didn't know that?"

Kelly let the snide remark pass and kept to the point. "She doesn't get to dictate how life is going to work. Yes, she gets input. But she *doesn't* get the final say. When it's all said and done, we're the ones who say what's best for her."

He let his arms drop to his sides. At last. He even went over and sat on the edge of the bed. "She said she's really glad she found me, glad to have her dad back with her. But that she's been doing okay with just you and that brother of yours." He looked away. "She said her uncle Tanner's been like a dad to her...."

Suddenly, she ached for him. She wished there was something she could say that would make a difference right then. But since he pretty much considered her the enemy, she figured it was better if she just kept quiet.

A moment later, he continued, "Long and short? She's happy I'm here. She's sure we're going to get along fine. But when I mentioned her coming to stay with me, she wasn't going for it. She told me she had friends who live between two houses and they don't like it at all. She's happy with her house and her friends. She wants to be *here* on weekends and holidays. And she has two recitals coming up at her dance studio in the next month. And then there's the spring play at school. Rehearsals for that start in a week. Some of them are on Fridays after school, when she would be on a plane on her way to see me. She's very busy and she told me I should try and see that and not drag her away from her house and her mom and her dog." He sent her a wry glance. "She said since I'm rich and have a limo, I can just add a room onto your house and move in here. Then I can see her whenever I want to." His gaze found her again. He looked almost…vulnerable.

Kelly had to remind herself—again—that showing him any sympathy was only asking for rejection. "Mitch. You have to give her a little more time…"

"Yeah. I know it. As soon as she stopped telling me how she was living here and that was that, I explained that I'm her parent and the parent is the one who decides how things work out. Then she said, 'For a new daddy, you are very bossy. And I don't want to go live in some strange place half of the time.'" He raked his hands back through his thick hair. "I didn't get through. She just doesn't want to live anywhere but here."

"Look. You can't expect her to just jump at the chance to turn her life upside-down. Time. That's what you both need. You can…go ahead with your book tour. You can call. Often. And visit her, of course. And then, when we think you're both ready for more, we can set up a time when she comes to visit you. And then take it from there, you know? Just…work into it. Slowly."

He braced his elbows on his spread knees and stared at the bedside rug between his feet. "I'm sorry. I can't. I can't do that. I can't leave. Not yet."

"Oh, no. Mitch, I am getting a very bad feeling here."

He lifted his head and met her eyes. "I'm going to have to stay here. For a while longer. I know you don't like it. I don't like it, either. But I need more time with her in her own environment, before I drag her off to live in some strange place she's never been before."

"No," she said. "No, it just won't work. And how can you keep staying here, anyway? You have two businesses to run and you're supposed to be on a book tour."

"I told you, I already cancelled the tour. I wrote the book to help people, anyway, to share what I know about how to live a more successful life. If it doesn't sell another damn copy, I couldn't care less. And both of my businesses are set up so they can run without a lot of hands-on attention from me. That's how I operate. I give a hundred and ten percent during start-up, and then, as time goes on, I let my people run the show. That frees me up to move on to the next project."

"The next project being your daughter?"

His lip curled. It wasn't a smile. "That was low."

She copped to it. "All right. Sorry. It's only… Well, it's impossible, having you here. You and I just don't get along. With you around, I'm on edge all the time. I refuse to live like that in my own house."

He hung his head again, that comma of dark hair falling forward in front. The seconds ticked by. And then, when he finally looked up, she knew she was in big trouble.

For the first time since the night she told him he had a daughter, he spoke to her gently. "I'll clean up my act. I promise you. I'll be helpful and I'll…get along with you."

And make her want to have wild sex with him even more than she already did? Gee. How terrific was that? "It won't work."

"It will. I'll see to it. I know it's been difficult—that I've been hard on you. But it will be better. You'll see. And you and I need to learn to get along, anyway. After all, we're going to be raising the same kid."

"For how long would you stay here?" Gaaa. Had she actually said that?

"I can't say. Yet. But not that long. Until I feel I'm on a better footing with her, until it's not all so strange and new between us. I need to be comfortable with her, and she needs to be comfortable with me. I need to learn to be a real father to her…."

"Yes. I know. But you don't have to move in here, to live in my house, to do that."

"Please, Kelly…"

Okay. She was certain about it now. She had *sucker* written across her forehead. "Oh, Mitch…"

He knew he was getting to her and he pressed his advantage. "I'll help out around here. Pull my weight. Pay my way, which goes without saying. I'm not much of a cook, but I can order some mean takeout. I'll get someone in to clean, keep the house. So you don't have to waste time on that. I'll—"

"Stop." She rubbed her temples. And gave it up. "The takeout now and then sounds tempting. But forget the housekeeper. I don't consider it a waste of time to clean my own house."

He leaned toward her, looking handsome and eager and absolutely delicious. "Whatever. I meant, if you need anything, if there's anything I can do to make your and DeDe's lives better and easier, consider it done. And as for my share of the living expenses…" He named a figure.

"That's way too much. Really."

"For DeDe, nothing's too much."

How could she argue with that? And why did he have to go and be civil with her? It wasn't fair. She liked it better when he acted like a jerk. Then she got so exasperated with him, she could almost forget that it was her job now to do what she could to facilitate her daughter's relationship with him.

"Come on," he said, all velvet-eyed charm now, reminding her like a jab to the heart of the wonderful man who'd sat across from her in the restaurant the other night, of the simple and joyous reunion they'd shared until...

If only she hadn't been pregnant when he cut her out of his life a decade before.

But no. If she hadn't been pregnant, there would be no DeDe. DeDe, with her shining eyes, her quick mind and her warm hugs and two left feet....

Worth any price.

"Just for a while..." he added.

"All right," she said. "I give, already. We'll try it." She stood.

He looked up at her. "Thank you."

There were a million things she might have said then.

She said none of them. She got the heck out of there.

The next day was Saturday. Mitch took DeDe to the zoo and then to a movie. In the evening, she had a sleepover party at a friend's house. He drove her there.

He didn't return to the house until after ten. He'd been to Best Buy, he explained. The explanation was more or less unnecessary, as he brought in a plasma television with a Best Buy price tag taped to the box, as well as one of those printers that would also send a fax *and* a stand for his iPod. When you put the iPod in the stand, it acted like a stereo.

"For my room," he told her. "Sometimes I do need the use of a fax. And I notice there's a cable outlet in the room already for the TV. I hope this is all right."

"Of course. Why wouldn't it be?"

"Well, I also had to kind of buy a desk for my laptop and a stand for the printer—and also one for the television. Oh, and a desk chair. I needed, that, too."

She gave him a look. "You had to 'kind of buy'?"

He looked so sheepish. It was way too charming. "I mean, since space is at a premium in there, I had to find pieces that would fit. It wasn't easy."

"My heart goes out."

"The rest of what I bought is in the limo."

She realized he was still unsure if all the stuff was okay. "Hey. It's your room—I mean, for as long as you're here."

He smiled. Something inside her went all warm and fuzzy. "I was hoping you'd say that."

"And at least you didn't buy a bunch of expensive electronics for DeDe, thus totally spoiling her beyond all recognition."

"I was tempted, believe me. She doesn't even have an Xbox."

"Exactly. I don't want her sitting in front of a TV screen half the day, working out nothing but her thumbs."

"Ever heard of a Wii?"

"We?" She was teasing.

But he didn't realize it. "I'll explain later."

She let the Wii issue go. "Do you need help, bringing it all in?"

"John can help me—but there is some assembly required."

"I'm game."

So he and the limo driver brought in the furniture and took it to the bedroom. Mitch tipped the driver and let him go for the night.

Then Kelly helped him put the legs on the stands and on the desk, which was really just a table—it had no drawers. They hooked up the TV and set up the printer, which he would use with the laptop he already had.

Really, he did most of it. Once they got the legs on the desk, Kelly sat on the edge of the bed and watched him. It was…nice.

Nice. Who knew? He'd promised to change his attitude, but had she really believed him? Not until now, sitting on the edge of the bed, watching him hook up his new plasma TV.

"There." He grabbed the remote, dropped to the bed beside her and punched the power button. "So. What do think?"

"Lookin' good."

"Oh, yeah." He flipped through the channels.

"It's a really clear picture."

He turned his head her way and grinned.

She realized she was looking at his mouth. Bad idea. He was far too hunky and sexy and good-looking for her peace of mind. Best to get on out of there. She popped to her feet. "So. You're good to go…."

"You're leaving?" The way he looked at her, that dark hazel gaze making a slow pass down her body and back up again. Only one word for that: dangerous.

She nodded so hard she felt like a bobble-head doll. "Good night, then."

"Thanks."

"Uh. For what?"

"The help."

"Oh, that. Well. You're welcome." She fled.

In her room, she remembered she had to call Tanner. He didn't pick up, so she left a message reminding him of dinner at five the next night, and adding, trying her best to sound blasé, "And by the way, DeDe knows now that Mitch is her father. And Mitch and I have decided he'll be staying here for a while. It's open-ended. Please. Don't ask."

He called her back at ten Sunday morning. As luck would have it, she was alone. Mitch had gone to pick up DeDe up from her sleepover.

Tanner asked, "You sure you know what you're doing with this?"

"No. But that's how it is. I just want us all to get along."

Tanner chuckled. "Didn't somebody say that during the L.A. riots all those years ago?"

"It was Rodney King, I think. So?"

"Didn't have much of an effect, as I recall."

Chapter Eight

"Still a P.I., right?" Mitch asked.

Tanner, across the table, leveled a flat look at him. "That's right."

"So, how's business?"

"Just great. Bought your book. Lots of good advice in there."

"Thanks," said Mitch.

Kelly wracked her brain for something to say that would get the two men to stop eyeing each other like a pair of alpha dogs circling the same bone.

"Bought Kelly a copy, too," said Tanner. He

looked across at her, dark eyes revealing nothing. "It's on the table in the front hallway."

"Thanks," said Kelly with forced cheer. "I've been looking forward to reading it."

"Are you guys mad?" DeDe peered suspiciously from her uncle to her father and back to her uncle again.

Both men lied, "No, of course not," in unison.

"Well, you act like you're mad."

"DeDe," said Kelly, "eat your peas."

"But I hate peas."

"Eat them anyway."

Somehow, they got through the meal, after which DeDe suggested a game of Monopoly. Tanner suddenly realized he had somewhere else he had to be.

Kelly urged him to stay, but he said he really couldn't, so DeDe hugged her uncle, and Tanner and Mitch shared terse goodbyes.

Outside, Tanner leaned against the gleaming driver's door of the metallic black Mustang he drove when he wasn't working. "Great pork chops. As always."

She wrapped her cardigan closer around her to ward off the nighttime chill. "Wish you would stay."

"Look. Bad idea. I doubt seriously that Michael— er, Mitch, and I are ever going to be best friends."

"He's DeDe's dad."

"I know. And I'm dealing with that. I get that he's

got a right to his kid and she's got a right to her dad. But every time I look at him, I see the whiny, irresponsible jerk who turned his back on you when you didn't make the choice he wanted you to make, the kid who disappeared into nowhere and couldn't be found when you needed him most."

"Tanner. People change."

He looked down at his boots. "Yeah. You're right." He slanted her a glance. "And I did think his book was good. Inspiring, you know? And like I said before, money helps. And he's got plenty now. DeDe will benefit from that."

"Just…try again. Next Sunday? Dinner?"

"He's gonna be hanging around here that long?"

"Probably."

He looked at the concrete between his boots some more. Then finally said, "I'll be here."

"Thanks."

They shared a hug. He got in behind the wheel. She shut the door and stepped back. She watched him as he drove away, her shoulders hunched against the cold.

Inside, at the kitchen table, DeDe and Mitch were playing Monopoly. They invited her to join in.

She shook her head. "You two have fun."

She finished cleaning up the kitchen and then got Mitch's book from the hallway table and took it to her room. She read until DeDe tapped on her door to kiss her good-night.

The next week wasn't bad at all, really.

Mitch leased a Lexus so he could come and go—and ferry DeDe around—without having to call for a car.

Hayley called on Tuesday and Kelly brought her up to speed.

"You're kidding," her sister said. "He's *living* with you?"

"It's temporary."

"How long is that?"

"Hey. If I only knew."

"Are you sure about this—about him staying in your house?"

"Nope. Not in the least. But he deserves a chance to get to know DeDe."

"Of course he does. But there are other ways he could do that than moving in on you."

"Hayley. It's all right. I'm…okay with it."

"If you say so."

"I do," Kelly reassured her.

They talked for another half hour. "I'm here, if you need me," Hayley said at the end. "Just call."

"I know that. And thanks."

When Mitch wasn't watching one of DeDe's dance lessons or picking her up from a friend's house, he worked on his laptop or read or watched his fancy TV. He also joined a local gym and he went there every morning after DeDe left for school. And Kelly knew he spent at least a few hours a day on the phone, wheeling and dealing from his temporary "office" in the guest room.

Kelly had her own work to do. Nine to five she kept her mind on her job. She really only had intermittent contact with Mitch: in the early morning for a few minutes at the breakfast table and then over dinner. Later in the evening, after DeDe was in bed, they'd sometimes share a brief conversation—about how the day had gone, about how Mitch and DeDe were getting along.

Kelly kept those nightly talks brief. Mostly because she didn't want to get too…involved with him. He'd made it painfully clear that their only connection now was the child they shared. She told herself she was fine with that. Having Mitch in her house was totally doable—well, except for how she was always thinking about sex lately.

That was the hardest part, hands down, about being around him so much. The guy was only being agreeable to her because she'd insisted on it as a condition of his living in her home. She knew that.

She did. So how come she couldn't stop getting lost in wild fantasies of seeing him naked, of feeling his arms wrapped tight around her, of the two of them, rocking it slow and easy in her bed? Or his bed. Or the sofa, the kitchen table, the family room easy chair…

A sex life. She really needed one. If she had one, she just knew she wouldn't be so fixated on Mitch as a sexual partner.

And the strange thing, the really worrisome thing, was that now and then she'd catch him looking at her in that certain way, a way that made her wonder if maybe he had a few fantasies of his own….

Dangerous ground. Oh, yeah. Complications they really didn't need.

But it was okay, she kept telling herself. Neither of them had done a thing about making their fantasies into reality—and neither of them would.

Saturday, DeDe had another sleepover—this time, a birthday slumber party. Mitch drove her there at five, with her backpack full of pj's, her toothbrush and toothpaste and a brightly wrapped birthday gift cradled in her arms.

Kelly had kissed her goodbye and then returned to her office to finish paying the bills.

Mitch was back in no time. She heard him come in, his footsteps going by outside her office door on the way to his own room.

She finished with the bills and then sat back in her desk chair and pondered the evening to come.

If only Hayley still lived in town. She would have

called her, asked her if she could get Marcus, her husband, to do babysitting duty, maybe meet Kelly for a burger and a movie—and yes, there were other women she could call. Friends from work, friends who had kids DeDe's age, friends from college.

But no. She wasn't really in the mood to hang out with anyone but her sister. With Hayley, she could talk freely about whatever was on her mind. With a friend, well…

Maybe not.

It was six-fifteen. She'd bought some scallops of veal that afternoon at the market, thinking maybe she'd make veal piccata tomorrow when Tanner came for dinner. But she'd also bought a brisket. Tanner loved brisket.

So. She'd do the veal tonight, open that bottle of sauvignon blanc she'd stuck in the fridge weeks ago and never got around to opening.

If Mitch wanted to join her, well, why not?

Dangerous, whispered the voice of wisdom from somewhere way in the back of her mind.

Kelly ignored that voice and headed for the kitchen.

"What's going on in here?"

She glanced over her shoulder. He stood in the doorway to the dining room in khakis, mocs and a soft sweater. The usual thrill went zipping through her. She pretended not to feel it.

"Veal piccata," she said. "Just pounding the veal scallops—but lightly. No need to beat them to death. You staying in tonight?"

"Yeah. I was just thinking about whether to have Chinese or ribs, but now you mention veal…I really like veal."

She sent him a wry look. "You like everything."

"True. But especially veal piccata. Can't beat that amazing lemon flavor."

"Well, then maybe you should join me for dinner."

"You're on. What can I do to help?"

She tipped her head toward the bottle of wine on the end of the counter. "Open that. Set the table…."

Ten minutes later, they were clinking their wine-glasses. "To the chef," he said.

"I'll drink to that." She sipped. "Hmm. Pretty good."

"*Very* good," he corrected.

"A sturdy little table wine," she said.

He laughed. "If you say so."

It was a one-course deal. Salad, pasta, the veal in its savory lemon sauce and the bread served together. He said it was all fantastic and she smiled modestly. Then, for a few minutes, neither of them spoke, except to ask for the bread basket or the butter.

It was natural, she supposed, that they'd start talking of the past.

He said, "I remember you were always a good cook."

She buttered a roll. "Some of my foster moms, their idea of dinner was a quick trip to the drive-through for burgers and fries. They liked it when I cooked. And I liked it when they were happy with me. But it was always simple stuff. Casseroles, things with ground beef. Good, basic food. Cheap food. My foster mothers weren't wasting their hard-earned cash on pricey cuts of meat or expensive condiments." She set down her butter knife. "Cheap and basic. That's pretty much my style to this day, I admit. Though occasionally I'll splurge on a quality cut of veal."

He cut a bite of meat, dredged it in the sauce and ate it slowly. "You made Thanksgiving dinner, re-member? Bought all the stuff and brought it over to the trailer and did it up right. I was so impressed. It was really good."

"Your mom was so sweet," she said.

"She was grateful that you pulled a real Thanks-giving together. After my dad left us, she just didn't have the heart for things like holiday dinners."

Kelly laughed. "What a group, huh? Your mom, so sad and distant. My mom, pretty much a basket case, whining the whole time about how she should have cooked the dinner, but she couldn't, she'd just lost her job again…."

"And you and me. Young and in love without two cents to our names." He looked at her over the rim of his wineglass. "We had some good times."

"Oh, yeah. We did…."

The glance they shared lasted way too long. She knew it. She truly did.

But somehow, she couldn't drag her gaze away.

He said, "My junior prom…"

"God. How could I forget?" That had been their first big date. She was a sophomore that year and she'd noticed him in the halls. He'd had long hair and he always wore black. People said he was trouble.

And his reputation only made him more attractive to her. Even to the prom, he'd worn his trademark black: a black suit and dress shirt and a black tie. She'd thought he looked so mysterious and sexy.

She said, "I always wondered where you got that black suit."

He considered, then shrugged. "It would have killed me to admit it then, but I guess there's no harm in telling you now. The Salvation Army."

Tenderness welled. "Oh, Mitch…" She made herself look away, ate more veal, twirled pasta on her fork. Sipped her wine. Once she felt she could look at him without getting teary-eyed, she said, "You had that ancient Chrysler New Yorker then, remember?"

"That car was over twenty years old at the time." He said it proudly.

She added, "Which is probably why it finally gave up the ghost, and we had to take the bus or hitch a ride to see each other."

"But that night," he said, "we had the New Yorker and we went in style. You wore that red velvet dress…."

"Burgundy velvet. I made it myself. My home-ec teacher let me use one of the school sewing machines. I chose the pattern because it was A-line. Simple."

"Whatever. You were beautiful. I remember my first sight of you in that dress. Blew me away."

She laughed. "Oh, I remember, too. The TV was on full blast in the living room and my foster mom, Reena, was yelling at her boyfriend to turn it down. One of the babies was screaming…."

"Didn't hear any of it. You opened that door. I saw you. That's all she wrote."

"Oh, my," she said softly. "It seems so long ago. Were we ever that young?"

"Apparently so."

The eye contact was getting seriously out of hand. She found herself glancing from his eyes to his mouth and back again. He was doing the same.

So what? She savored another slow sip of wine. "This is…good. You and me. Reminiscing. Remembering how it was. A lot of ugly stuff happened. But we did have…love. So deep and passionate."

He agreed. "We did."

"And even though it didn't work out between us, well, I'm glad for what we had. And what we made. DeDe. I'm grateful every day for her."

He said, "Yeah. She's something. She's the best." He raised his glass again. "To DeDe."

Kelly added, "And to how it was. In the good times." Their glasses touched with a bright, hopeful chime of sound.

In the corner, Candy's hind leg thumped the floor. She woofed softly and then let out a low whine. Kelly glanced over. The dog was sound asleep. Probably dreaming whatever an old dog dreams. Of chasing a rabbit, of treeing the neighbor's cat...

When she looked at Mitch again, she found he was watching her.

"I shouldn't say this." He spoke low.

Then don't, she should have answered. But she didn't. She only stared into his eyes and waited for him to say the rest.

He did. "We made love after that dance, re-member? For the first time. In the backseat. I almost died when I saw your breasts. Not to mention the rest of you...in the moonlight."

The memory claimed her: his face above her, so full of longing. And love. She'd felt it, too, so intensely—the longing, the need. The absolute certainty that this was love and it would last them forever. She had cried out as he filled her for the very first time….

She said, "It was so…scary. I remember I felt completely out of my depth. We didn't have a clue what we were doing, really. Just letting nature take its course." She realized she was whispering. Somehow, it didn't seem the kind of memory they could recall in everyday voices.

He almost smiled, the corners of his beautiful mouth tipping upward oh-so-slightly. "So you were scared, huh?"

"Oh, yeah. You?"

"Truth?"

"Absolutely."

He confessed, "I was flat-out terrified."

She laughed. "Exactly. Me, too."

"But at the same time, I was so damned excited. I couldn't believe it was really happening."

"Yes. I know. I was scared to death. And yet…it was so special. So…right."

"I was afraid I had hurt you."

"You did. But I wanted it. I wanted…you."

"I want you now," he said.

For a split second she was certain she hadn't heard him right. She swallowed, licked her lips. Her stomach had hollowed out and her heart was bonging away like a gong under her breasts.

Time to stop this craziness. But instead, she said, "I want you, too. I can't stop thinking about it, about us. Making love together. Again."

"Neither can I."

"I want your hands on me. I want to feel you on top of me, inside of me... Oh, God. Why are we talking about this?" She set down her napkin, pushed to her feet.

He stood, as well.

They faced each other across the table. He watched her, his big body gathered as if to strike. And her body? Aching. For his touch, for his kisses.

She knew she should turn and run. And she hoped, if she did, he would stop her.

"We can't be considering this," she whispered.

His eyes were dark, shadowed, intense. "Where else could it go? After all these years. After...what we had. And who does it hurt? No one. We're both single. DeDe's gone for the night. We're here in your house alone together and what we do tonight is our business. No one's going to judge us for it."

"But you...you don't even like me anymore, Mitch. You're so angry with me. It doesn't seem right. To make love with a man who doesn't even like me anymore."

"Truth?"

"Please."

"Yeah. I'm still angry. But I see the way you

are…around here, with DeDe. Just as a person. You're helpful. Generous. Smart. Patient. You never complain, you just do what needs doing and move on. I can't help but like you. Admire you, even."

A warm flush crept up her cheeks. His words gave her great pleasure. But no way could she miss the deeper, negative meaning beneath them. "Listen to yourself. You *can't help* but like me. Meaning you have no choice?"

"There's always a choice." He spoke the words roughly.

"Exactly. And what you're really saying is that you don't trust me and, in your heart, you resent me. You feel I kept your child from you. You can never forgive me for that."

"That is not what I said."

"But it is what you *meant*. Oh, Mitch. I just don't know…."

"Yeah. You do. You know." He set his napkin down. "But I'm not pushing you into anything. Thanks for an excellent dinner. Honestly. It was really good."

She let him get as far as the doorway to the formal dining room before she said, "Wait."

Chapter Nine

She groaned when he touched her.

Mitch drank in that hungry, womanly sound. He wrapped his arms around her and pulled her to him. Hard. She'd been driving him nuts, making him crazy. For over a week now.

Living in her house and keeping his hands off her…talk about impossible.

He'd told himself to get the hell over it. That he wouldn't have her, that she wouldn't have him. That it was for the best, anyway. The situation was tough enough, an affair with her would only make it more so.

So much for getting over it.

He bent his head and took her mouth, drinking in her sigh of surrender as he licked the maddening cupid-bow shape of those amazing lips of hers.

"Oh," she said. "Oh, Mitch. Yes…"

He caught her upper lip, sucked it gently, then speared his tongue inside. She moaned some more and pressed that pretty, soft body against him, so tight. So good.

She was…a dream, lost. A dream surrendered, one he'd never again hoped to find. He couldn't love her. Not anymore.

But he couldn't get her off his mind, either.

She got to him.

She turned him inside out in ways no other woman had come close to doing. He'd been aroused since they started talking about their first time, in the backseat, after the prom. Hard and getting harder as each second ticked by.

He cupped her bottom and pressed that hardness into her lower belly, closing his eyes, a deep groan escaping him.

This was really happening. Him and Kelly. After way too many long, lonely years.

She let him have her tongue to suck. He did, rhythmically, in long, hard draws, swirling his own tongue around it. All the while, he was breathing in through his nose, filling himself with the scent of her, a scent long-remembered, though he'd tried to forget it: sweet. Womanly. Slightly musky with desire.

Perfect for him.

But then she pulled away.

He tried to recapture the kiss, to claim those tempting lips again, to have her body pressed tight to his once more.

But she was pushing at his shoulders, saying his name. "Mitch…"

He swore. "What?"

"I don't have anything…for contraception."

"No problem. I do." He reclaimed that soft mouth of hers, at the same time as he hitched her body up good and close. The feel of her round bottom in his hands…was there anything to match that?

Well, maybe the taste of her. That was right up there, another peak life experience, best of the best.

He speared his tongue in, tasting her fully.

Kissing Kelly again.

At last.

He'd actually believed that it wasn't going to happen.

Who had he thought he was kidding? There was no denying this.

And she had too many clothes on. He caught her by the waist and put her away from him.

She looked up at him, head lolling back on the

stem of her neck. "What? Mitch…please…" She clutched his shoulders, tried to pull him close again.

"Oh, yeah," he whispered. "You knew it would happen. You knew it *had* to happen…."

"Yes. I knew. I did."

"From the moment I saw you again, standing there on that stage."

"Oh. Oh, yes…"

"Do something for me."

"Yes. All right…"

"Take off your clothes."

She sighed, straightened her shoulders and blinked at him lazily, like a woman waking from a long, drugged sleep. "Here? Now?"

"Yeah."

And then she smiled, a smile that made him ache to kiss those lips again. "One condition."

He traced a finger along the firm line of her jaw. The simple touch aroused him. Everything about her aroused him. After all these years, it was just like it had been when they were kids—only more so. He answered roughly, "I can guess."

She told him anyway. "You have to take your clothes off, too."

As if that was a tough deal to make. "You got it."

"Race you."

Had he known that was coming? "Say when."

She dropped her hands from his shoulders and

took one step back. He did the same, thinking of the love games they used to play back in the day. Once they'd gotten past the awkwardness of those first few times, they'd found a certain freedom with each other. To tease. To draw out the pleasure with a little innocent fun and games.

She had her hands at her sides and she was flexing her fingers. She rolled her neck, like an athlete loosening up for the first burst of speed off the line.

He grunted. "Oh, come on."

She laughed. And then, out of nowhere said, "Go for it!"

He grabbed his sweater, ripped it up and over his head. He dropped it at the same time as she dropped hers.

In unison, they unbuttoned buttons, tore zippers wide. He skimmed down his khakis, kicked them away, followed by his mocs. She shed her flat shoes and jeans. All he had left were his boxers.

He waited, grinning like a fool, as she jumped on one foot and then the other, getting off her socks.

She stood tall. In little white panties and a white bra to match. Her breasts, not large, yet fuller than he remembered, plumped above the cups of the bra. He ached to touch them at last, to feel that silky, giving flesh.

She pursed up her lips and braced her fists on

her hips. "If you just stand there staring at me, it's not a race."

"To hell with the race. Take off that bra."

She slanted him a glance, purely feminine, meant to taunt him. "Say please."

"Take it off."

She slipped one strap down her arm. And then the other. And then she had the nerve to bat her eyelashes. "Excuse me?"

"Off."

"DeDe was right."

"What are you talking about?"

"You are bossy. You were always bossy. You realize that, don't you?"

"What part of *off* was unclear to you?"

She fluttered her eyelashes some more and heaved a big, fake sigh. He couldn't help but admire the slender shape of her shoulders, the feminine musculature of her slim arms, the way her waist curved maddeningly inward. She said, "You should take off those boxers first, I think."

With his thumbs, he hooked the elastic around his waist. "And when I do?"

"The bra goes next."

"Promise?"

"Promise."

He didn't believe her. Still, he played fair. One of them had to. He eased the waistband over his erection, shoved the boxers down and stepped out of them. He stood tall. "Satisfied?"

She widened her eyes, licked her lips. "I know that I will be."

"The bra," he reminded her.

"Like I said, you are much too bossy." She sounded somewhat breathless. "But you do look amazing without your clothes. There's definitely something to be said for a guy who works out…."

"The bra."

"Oh. That's right…" She reached behind her. He heard the hooks snap free. He groaned.

"What was that?" she asked sweetly.

He muttered a very bad word.

"You never did say please…."

"Cheater," he accused.

"Please?" she suggested.

"Kelly, you know you're not playing fair."

"Please?"

He swore again. She clucked her tongue at him. And he couldn't take it anymore. He gave her what she wanted, gruffly. "Please."

"Oh. Well." She shifted her shoulders. Just slightly. "Since you ask me so nicely…" The straps slid the rest of the way down her arms and the bra dropped to the kitchen floor.

In the corner, the old dog went, "Woof," in its sleep.

He said, "Kelly…"

And she said, "Mitch."

And then they were reaching for each other. She came into his arms, all smooth, willing softness. She offered her mouth and he claimed it. And then he took her by the waist and lifted her high. She wrapped her legs around him. He went on kissing her as he carried her.

She opened her eyes wide, let out a sweet, soft, "Oh!" of surprise as he set her on the jut of counter to the left of the sink. "What…?"

"Shh…" He kissed her some more as he explored her, cupping those beautiful breasts, skimming the nipples with the pads of his thumbs, caressing his way downward along the curving shape of her rib cage.

His fingers brushed the elastic top of her panties. He eased a finger under, to pet the silky flesh of her hip.

She shuddered and moaned.

He got hold of the panties on either side. "Lift up…."

She braced her hands on the counter and lifted her bottom enough that he could slide the panties off. He guided them down her pretty legs and off over her red-tipped toes, letting them drop to the floor by the table.

"Come here," she pleaded, reaching out her arms. "Here to me…"

He was only too happy to move in close again.

He eased himself between her thighs. And then he kissed her again, a leisurely kiss, as burning hot as it was slow and deep. She'd always been an incredible kisser. He could almost feel the steam shooting out of his ears.

He lifted his mouth, then, just enough so he could speak, and he whispered against her parted lips, "You drive me crazy. You always did…."

She let out a small, eager cry and started kissing him again. Her hands were all over him, sliding along his shoulders, up into the close-cut hair at the nape of his neck, then around to the front of him, over his pecs and down toward where he was pointing due north.

He groaned hard and loud when she wrapped those fingers of hers around him. She moaned in response, fingers tightening as, with her thumb, she rubbed the tip.

"You're killing me…" he muttered.

"That was the plan." Her breath was sweet, her lips tempting him to take another kiss.

He took it, as she began to stroke him.

It was heaven, those fingers of hers, working the magic that she'd always worked so well. He let her have her way with him, allowing his head to fall back, the groans rumbling up from deep within—until he knew he would lose it if she dared one more stroke.

He caught her wrist.

She moaned in protest at losing her prize, but she

did take his signal. With a final reluctant squeeze, she let him go.

He kissed the side of her neck. She tipped her head for him, exposing the sleek flesh for him to caress. He licked his way downward, enjoying her gasps of pleasure, as he dipped his tongue in the tender groove where her collarbones met.

She clutched his shoulders, lifting her breasts for him. He took them in his mouth to suck, one and then the other, catching the hard nipples between his teeth, working them lightly. Her body shuddered in his arms.

He trailed his tongue down the center of her chest, over the slight softness of her belly— testament, he knew, to the child they had made. She clutched his head between her hands and said his name, over and over, like a plea. He kissed her navel, ran his tongue around it in a slow circle, then blew where he'd licked to feel her shiver and beg him for more.

"Oh, Mitch. Yes. Please, please…"

He was only too happy to give her just what she was asking for. One hand on either of her smooth thighs, he eased them still wider apart. And then he bent lower, to nuzzle the softly curling hair over her mound. He put his hand on her, eased her open with a gentle thumb.

So wet.

So ready…

He scented her. Musky. Achingly sweet. And then he tasted her. She cried out at the feel of his tongue, there, where she was so wet. So ready for him. He lowered himself to his knees for better access and she scooted closer, to the edge of the counter.

She murmured broken, tender words, her hands in his hair, holding on as he kissed her, sliding his fingers up from underneath so he could stroke her with them, as well as his tongue.

In no time, she was quivering, reaching the crest. With a low cry, she found what she was seeking. He felt the spill of greater wetness as she came, and then the pulsing. The taste of her was as sweet as honey. He kissed her, an endless kiss, lasting 'til the moment when her body went lax. She drooped against the cabinet behind her.

He looked up at her. She was so beautiful in her satisfaction.

"Oh," she said, her pretty breasts shining with a light sheen of sweat, rising and falling as she gulped in hard, panting breaths. "Oh, well. That was… amazing…."

He wanted her mouth again. He wanted all of her. He rose, moving up her body, until he could kiss her, deeply.

She accepted the kiss, parting her lips for him, draping lazy arms on his shoulders, letting him have her mouth to do what he would with it.

It was good, to kiss her. But it wasn't enough. He wanted to feel her all around him. But he needed to deal with contraception first.

He said, between quick, brushing kisses, "I want you right here. On this counter…"

"Oh," she said. "Yes. That would be just fine. Beds are so…ordinary, aren't they?"

"Well, I like a bed. A bed is fine. Anywhere is fine."

She chuckled, the sound like a purr against his mouth. "Spoken like a man."

"Men are basic. Pragmatic."

"Oh, Michael…"

"Mitch."

"That's right. Mitch. Michael. Either. Both."

He caught her lower lip between his teeth and sucked on it. Gently.

"Oh," she said. "That. Yes…"

"If I go and get the condoms, will you promise to stay right here?"

She laughed the laugh of a satisfied woman. "Like I could move if I wanted to."

"Is that a yes?"

"Yes. It's a yes." She sagged against the cabinet again. "But hurry back."

"Count on it." Reluctantly, he left her, taking off down the hall, grabbing what he needed from the drawer in his room.

When he returned to her, he found that she'd

kept her promise. She sat on the counter, right where he'd left her. "Well, that was fast."

"I got two. Just in case."

"I like a man who plans ahead."

He dropped one of the packets on the table and unwrapped the other one. He rolled it down over himself.

She was watching, a funny look on her face.

He said, "Okay. It was like this." He moved in close, kissed her temple, pressed his lips to her silky hair and whispered in her ear, "A week ago? The night I bought the TV for my room?"

"Yeah?"

"I realized that night. If I got the chance with you, like this, I was going to want to be ready. So I went out and bought a box of these."

"Ah," she said, a sigh and an affirmation, at the same time.

"Scoot toward me." He cupped her bottom with one hand. With the other, he positioned himself.

She moaned. "Oh. It feels…"

He finished for her. "So good."

"So good." She moaned as he filled her, reaching for him, pulling him so close, wrapping her arms and her legs tight around him.

"Kelly. Move with me. Come with me…."

"Oh, yes…"

It was magic. The way it had been all those years ago. Magic. Burning hot and bright. Even after so much time apart, she somehow knew his rhythms as he knew hers. She picked up his cues and she gave them back to him. Her slightest sigh, her smallest moan—he knew them. Read them. Answered in kind.

More than once, he had to stop it, hold absolutely still. To keep from going over too soon. He wanted it to last.

She was hot and wet around him, and she clutched him so close. She whispered, "Yes. Oh, yes…like that. Oh, yeah…"

And he couldn't help himself. He was moving again, pressing in deep, letting himself out by slow degrees.

Until the slowness itself drove him wild and he had to up the tempo. She followed. She went with him. Willingly, eagerly, wherever he took her.

At the end, even stillness couldn't keep his climax from happening. He tried it anyway—stopped, waited, panting, pressing his forehead to hers, looking down at the place where they were joined, hoping the rising tide of his release would ebb, let him have a little more of this, let it go on just a little bit longer…

But it wasn't to be.

"I can't…" The words found their way up from the deepest part of him.

"Oh…" She moaned. "I know. Me, neither…"

He surrendered to it, pushing in so deep, giving her all of him, as she pressed herself against him, lifting her hips to him, offering everything.

He took it. All she had. And she held him tight on a low, keening moan. The end rolled through him, wiping out everything but the feel of her, the pulsing of her slick inner muscles around him as she hit the peak, too.

He cried her name.

And she moaned, "Yes…"

And then there was nothing, only the wave of sensation, rising higher, crashing over them, wiping out everything but the ecstasy of release.

Chapter Ten

Kelly woke early the next morning. For those first few seconds, as her mind shed the final cobwebs of sleep, it was like any other Sunday morning in recent years. The light that crept in between the shut blinds was grayish.

And she heard rain, didn't she? Drumming the roof, bouncing down the gutter pipe beside her bedroom window. A rainy Sunday. DeDe was at Devon Marie's birthday sleepover. Mitch would pick her up at...

Mitch.

Oh. My. God.

They *had*, hadn't they? She lay very still, hardly daring to breathe, images of the night before popping and flashing in her mind: on the kitchen counter. And then…on the dryer. While it was running.

She'd whispered how she'd always fantasized about doing it there. And he was only too willing to help her with that.

And then in her shower. They'd started out just wanting to freshen up a little. But even that had turned into love play.

After which, they'd ended up here.

In her bed.

Did this make her the definition of *stupid,* or what?

As if things weren't difficult enough already, with him insisting on believing she'd kept his child from him, with him admitting he *admired* her, but only because he couldn't help himself.

Had she jumped on the fast track to heartache?

No need to even answer that one.

She suppressed a sigh.

Then again…

A smile tried to pull at the corners of her mouth. Because. Really. How long had it been? Years. Since she'd felt a man's hands on her, since she'd given herself over to a fine time in bed.

Or out of it, for that matter.

And that time three years ago, the one time with a man other than Michael? Well, it hadn't been all that great, really. A single mom with a demanding job just didn't have all that much opportunity to go hunting down lovers, to indulge herself in romantic, sexy evenings for two.

She needed to get out more. She honestly did. As this little…lapse of judgment with Mitch had shown her all too clearly.

Slowly, she turned her head. Yep. There he was. So manly and hunky it hurt to look at him. Lying beside her in her bed.

As she stared at him, wondering why he couldn't just do her a favor and be less attractive, he opened those eyes that still, on occasion, haunted her dreams. "Good morning," he said.

"'Morning."

He frowned. "Is it raining?"

"Yeah."

And then he smiled.

And she smiled, too.

And when he reached for her, she went to him, turning, tucking herself against him, her back to his front. She drifted toward sleep again.

Until he cupped her breast.

A lovely, sensual warmth stole through her.

She sighed. He nuzzled her ear.

"Oh, Mitch," she whispered. "What are we doing?"

His only answer was, "Shh…"

* * *

What are we doing? The question cycled in Kelly's dazed brain all day. *What are we doing?*

She'd had wild, uninhibited sex with Mitch. Repeatedly. It had been amazing. And it had to stop.

But as soon as she'd think how it had to stop, she'd find herself smiling like a dreamy fool, remembering the feel of him, inside her, the taste of him on her tongue, the rough rumble of his voice in her ear, saying things that made her blush, things that made her beg for more.

And as soon as she started thinking how good it was, well, she couldn't help but move on to how, really, who would it hurt, how could it matter in the greater scheme of things if they did it again?

Again. And again…

Another issue: Way too many rooms in her house reminded her of the night before. The kitchen. The bedroom. Her bathroom…

And oh, God, the laundry room. After last night, she'd never think of her dryer in quite the same way. Since it was Sunday and Sundays she did laundry, she spent a lot of time in there that day. In the afternoon, when she transferred the final load to the dryer and turned it on, she lingered there with her hand on it, feeling the warmth and the steady vibration, remembering…

"Mom!"

"Oh!" She whipped her hand behind her back and whirled to face her daughter, who stood in the doorway from the kitchen, looking distinctly annoyed. Kelly coughed to clear the guilty lump from her throat. "What?"

DeDe scowled. "I said 'Mom' twice. You just stood there, staring at the wall, smiling…"

"Sorry. Really. What do you need?"

"My room. Remember? You sent me in there to clean it?"

"Well, yes. Of course, I remember. And did you?"

"Yes."

"Good, honey. Really good…"

"You want to check it?" DeDe eyed her sideways, as if worried about her sanity.

"Does it need checking?"

"Well, no."

"Okay, then. As long as it's clean…" Kelly started folding the linens she'd taken out of the dryer before putting that final load in, her mind already drifting back to what had happened last night.

"Mom?" DeDe hadn't budged from the doorway.

"Um, hmm? What?"

"Since my room's all done and I don't have any homework, can Dad and me play Wii bowling?"

The Wii. Kelly smiled dreamily. Mitch had been great about that, really. He could have showered

DeDe with expensive gifts. But he actually seemed to understand that buying her any pricey toy that caught her eye wouldn't be good for her—or their relationship. He'd bought the Wii last week, after Kelly had grudgingly given permission, with the understanding that DeDe would always do her chores and homework before they played.

"Mom?" DeDe was still waiting for an answer. "Can we?"

"Sure." Kelly snapped a towel.

"O-kay!" DeDe was off like a shot. Kelly folded the towel and reached for the next one, thinking, *What are we doing? It has to stop....*

As planned, Tanner came to dinner. He ate two helpings of brisket and asked her if she was feeling all right.

"Fine. Great. Really." She was scrupulously careful, as she had been all day, not to glance in Mitch's direction.

Tanner frowned. And then he shrugged. And then he said, "Pass the rolls."

Kelly thought that, on the whole, the dinner went well. Better than the week before. Tanner and Mitch weren't falling all over each other with mutual affection or anything, but they were civil enough, the sharp edge of shared hostility dulled at least a little. Tanner even stayed after dessert for a rousing game of Wii Mario Party 8.

It was still raining when he headed for his car at eight-thirty. DeDe hugged him goodbye, and Kelly walked him out as far as the front porch.

As soon as they were out the door, he caught her arm. "So okay. Tell me now. What's going on around here?"

Oh, right. Like she was going to explain to her overprotective big brother about having sex on the dryer with Mitch. "Tanner. Stop. Everything's okay— well, I mean, as okay as it can be given the situation."

He shook his head. "How long is he staying?"

"It's—"

"Let me guess. Open-ended, right?"

"That's right."

He turned and stared out through the veil of the rain, in the direction of his Mustang parked at the curb. "You guys getting back together?"

Her pulse was racing. Stupid, stupid. "No. Why?"

"I don't know. Just the vibe you two give off, I guess. You don't look at him—and he's *always* looking at you."

"Uh. He is?" Why did she have to sound so ridiculously hopeful?

Tanner faced her again. "He seems to be doing okay with DeDe." He said the words grudgingly, making it clear that he hadn't completely forgiven Mitch for the selfish boy he'd been once.

"She loves her new daddy," Kelly said. "And he thinks the sun rises and sets on her. It's all good."

"You sure about that?"

"Well, good enough. She's got him wrapped around her pinky finger, but I suppose that's to be expected."

He squeezed her shoulder. "Call me. If there's anything…"

"You know I will."

Inside, she found Mitch waiting in the hallway. She focused on a point beyond his shoulder. "DeDe?" she asked.

"Taking a bath."

"Great." She detoured through the living room to the kitchen, where the dishwasher would be ready for unloading by now.

He followed her. She considered turning to face him again, asking him to please keep his distance.

But in the end, she just kept walking.

In the kitchen, he hung back by the table. "You're avoiding me," he said.

She opened the dishwasher and pulled out the flatware basket. "Here. Make yourself useful."

In an edgy silence, they put the dishes away.

"Great," she said, when the dishwasher was empty. She closed the door. "Thanks."

"Glad to help." He was standing directly in her path.

She did the looking-past-his-shoulder thing and waited for him to go away. He didn't.

Instead, he moved in closer.

Every nerve in her body seemed to be quivering. What was up with that?

He whispered, "Tonight…"

"Oh, no, Mitch. Really. I don't think that's such a good…"

He touched her and she forgot how to speak. He brushed the side of her neck with the back of his fingers. And then he was, somehow, even closer. Close enough that she felt his body heat. "We'll talk."

That made her laugh. Which was good, really. It kind of broke the tension a little. "Oh, yeah, right." What she saw in his eyes had nothing to do with talking. "Not a good idea, Mitch. And you know it's not."

He brushed the side of her neck again, the touch so light, the intent so very clear. "As soon as DeDe's in bed."

The hour between the encounter in the kitchen and DeDe's bedtime seemed to crawl by.

Mitch tucked DeDe in. Kelly sat on the straight chair in the far corner of her own bedroom, fully dressed with the door shut, hoping against hope that Mitch would decide she'd meant what she said in the kitchen, that he'd go on to his own room without stopping to knock.

Two soft raps on the door told her that her hope was futile. Maybe if she just sat there and did nothing…

Didn't work. He knocked again. She got up on shaky legs and went to answer, opening the door only partway. "Mitch, really," she whispered. "This isn't a good idea."

He didn't budge. "Let me in."

"Only to talk…"

"Whatever you say."

So she stepped back and he stepped forward. He shut the door behind him.

"It's a bad idea," she told him, backing away until she reached the nightstand and had nowhere else to go.

He stayed by the door. "You already said that. In the kitchen."

"Uh, yes. I did. And I meant it. DeDe's nine. What if she walked in on us? What would she think?"

He looked her up and down, slowly. And way too thoroughly. "There is such a thing as locking the bedroom door."

"Mitch. Last night was…wonderful. But it shouldn't have happened. And it's not going to happen again. It's just…not wise. We've got enough problems to deal with now. And DeDe has to be the priority. And given that the two of us don't have any…future together, I can't see that spending our nights in bed together can lead anywhere but to trouble."

Okay, hard truth. She wanted him to tell her they did have a future together—or at least, maybe a chance for one.

"All right," he said. "If that's the way you want it, I understand."

Kelly got through the next few days, somehow. She and Mitch played it neutral with each other when DeDe was around. At night, Kelly went to her room and Mitch went to his. She didn't get much sleep that week. She spent most of each night lying awake, thinking about him.

Still, it was bearable.

More or less.

Except for the sleeplessness. And the tension that simmered just below the surface. Except for how she couldn't stop remembering in all-too-vivid detail the things they'd done on Saturday night. Except for the times when she would glance his way and find him watching her, and it would strike her like a blow straight to the heart. She wanted him so much, it hurt.

Except for all that, things were going okay.

Hayley called Thursday after DeDe was in bed. Kelly put a brave face on the situation—and didn't say a word about what had happened Saturday night. Sometimes, talking things out just wasn't the answer.

Hayley knew something was wrong, but she didn't press the point. She reminded Kelly again, "If you need me, call."

Kelly set the phone back on the nightstand and stared at the closed door of her bedroom. She longed to jump from the bed, fling open that door and run down the hall to Mitch's room.

As each day—each hour, each minute—passed, the truth became clearer. She would see him with DeDe, so patient and gentle. So full of love.

And she'd wish that he could be loving to her, too.

Now and then, even with all this tension between them, he'd say something funny, or perceptive or maybe just something nice about her cooking....

And her heart would ache. It was more than a physical thing, more than just the burning need to be with him again the way she had been Saturday night. She wanted...

The laughter. The sharing. The caring. She wanted to count on him. To have him count on her. She wanted to know that he would be there, beside her, as the years went by.

She wanted...

Mitch. All of him. In a forever kind of way.

Chapter Eleven

So much for sleeping.

Kelly did what she'd been doing most of the week, what people falling hopelessly in love tend to do; she tossed and turned all night. In the morning, she crawled out of bed and glared at herself in the bathroom mirror.

Ugh. She could play one of the zombies in *Dawn of the Dead*.

She showered and put on extra makeup to cover the dark circles under her eyes. Then she ate breakfast with her daughter and the man who had somehow managed to steal her heart for the second time.

"Rehearsal this afternoon?" Mitch asked their daughter.

The rehearsals for the spring play had started Monday. Mrs. Kendall, a drama buff who taught fifth grade, directed the play every year. She always chose something with a whole bunch of small parts, so any kid in the school who wanted to participate could have a role. This year they were doing an extravaganza called *Tales from the Brothers Grimm,* several short plays in one. DeDe, who loved acting almost as much as she loved to dance, had been given three roles: a witch, a princess and the back end of a unicorn.

"Yeah," DeDe said. "Rehearsal after school. And then I have to go to tap lessons after."

"No problem," Mitch told her. "I'll be there to drive you." The three of them ate in silence for few minutes. Then Mitch asked, "Well. Everything all right with Dustin now?"

Dustin Perry, an "older" boy, a fifth grader, played the front end of DeDe's unicorn. Since that first rehearsal Monday, she'd complained constantly about the boy, how she hated him, how he was such a creep, how he was always telling her what to do, bossing her around, calling her a brat. Mitch and Kelly had taken turns alternately consoling her and advising her not to let the boy get to her.

But then, last night, the whole evening had gone

by without DeDe once mentioning her frustrations with Dustin. Kelly had almost dared to hope her daughter was past that one.

No such luck. "I hate him," DeDe declared. "I hate him so much I don't even want to talk about him anymore. Ever." She resolutely shoved a big spoonful of cereal into her mouth and chewed with all her might.

Mitch frowned. "What did he do this time?"

DeDe swallowed hard. "Never mind."

"Come on." He looked at their child so tenderly. And in spite of all her frustrations with him, Kelly knew gladness, that her daughter had a father who cared, a father who would be there to help her grow up. "You can tell me," he coaxed. "I really want to know."

"Oh, Dad…"

"Come on."

DeDe sniffed. "He said he can't believe I could have taken all those dancing classes, because I've got two left feet and I can't even handle being the rear end of a unicorn." Her small mouth quivered. She stared down at her cereal, valiantly fighting back tears.

Mitch said, "Speaking of rear ends, you want me to kick his butt for you?"

DeDe's head snapped up. "Daaaad!"

"Just say the word." His eyes gleamed.

And the threat of tears vanished. DeDe giggled. "Oh, Dad. Of course not."

"Well, all right. His butt is safe from me. If that's how you want it, I mean. But remember…"

"What?"

"Anytime. You just say the word."

"Hitting people doesn't solve anything," DeDe told him loftily.

"Can't argue with that." Mitch lifted his coffee cup to her. "But always remember."

"What?"

"Dustin Perry doesn't know squat. You are absolutely perfect just the way you are."

"Oh, Dad…" DeDe's cheeks bloomed pink.

"Give that fool five years."

"You mean Dustin?"

"Yeah."

DeDe wrinkled up her nose. "Five years for what?"

"That's when he'll start coming around asking you to go out with him."

"Eewww. Dad. Gross."

Mitch grinned. "And that's when, if you still hate him, you'll get to tell him no."

It was stuff like that, the way he dealt with DeDe. So fondly. With such pride in her accomplishments, such total loyalty. But with a sense of humor, too.

How could Kelly help but fall in love with him again?

She drove to work on autopilot, thinking about him. Then, all through the morning staff meeting, she yo-yoed between longing for Mitch, and falling asleep.

In the breakroom at eleven, Renata told her she looked like hell and suggested she take the rest of the day off. "It'll be a major challenge, getting along without you for the next six hours. But trust me. We'll manage it somehow."

Kelly told the counselor she was fine, drank more coffee and went back to her office. By two that afternoon, though, even she had admit that she desperately needed a nap. She headed home—where she found a dusty red Camaro parked in her driveway.

At least the strange car was parked on Mitch's side. She pushed the remote button and the garage door rumbled up. The Lexus was there.

So…Mitch had company?

She pulled into her space, shut the door and went in through the laundry room, hearing Mitch's raised voice as she pushed the door inward.

"Damn it, Crystal. No. I don't want my cards read. And forget the massage."

A musical feminine voice argued, "But the tension is rippling off you in waves. I'm just trying to find some way to help you relax." Mitch had a woman here? Kelly's exhaustion evaporated, seared into oblivion by growing anger. How dare he bring another woman to *her* house?

She ought to storm in there and tell him…what?

Anything she said would just come out as a jealous rant. It wasn't as if she and Mitch were a couple or anything.

They weren't even temporary lovers. She herself had seen to that.

She shut the door. Quietly.

"I do not need to relax, damn it," boomed Mitch. "I need for you to tell me what the hell you're doing here."

Kelly hovered by the washer, hardly daring to breathe. The woman said something else, but Kelly couldn't make out the words. She tiptoed through the open doorway into the kitchen, placing the voices as she went. Mitch and the other woman were in the family room, beyond the dining room, at the back of the house.

Mitch said, "No. You're being ridiculous. All this woo-woo crap of yours drives me nuts. I'm fine. Seriously. I don't need your help. Just go back to L.A."

"You know I can't do that."

"Oh, but you can. You can and you will."

"I'm here for you, Mitch. Whether you admit that you need me or not, you're my brother. That's what matters."

Her *brother?* But Mitch didn't have a sister, except for Deirdre, who'd died all those years ago, did he?

"Don't start in with that you-are-my-brother stuff," Mitch commanded. "I do not want to hear it."

The musical voice replied, "Go ahead. Deny me. You are my brother and I know that you need me now. So I've sublet my apartment and I'm moving here, where I can help."

"Damn it. Don't help me, Crystal. Please. Anything but that."

It was all too weird for Kelly. As the woman began protesting again that she would help Mitch in spite of himself, Kelly stopped spying and started walking.

She marched through the dining room and stopped in the arch to the family room. "Ahem," she said.

Mitch turned to glare at her. "What are you doing home?"

She gave him a tight smile. "I was tired. I needed a nap. Strangely enough, though, I'm wide-awake now."

The woman named Crystal stood at the end of the sofa. She had long, curly golden hair and the face of an angel. "Hi. I'm Crystal. Crystal Cerise. You must be Kelly." She moved forward, extending her hand.

Good manners took over. Kelly walked toward the blonde. They met by the coffee table. Crystal captured her hand. They shook.

The blonde held on for a few seconds too long.

She stared into Kelly's eyes. "Oh," she said. "Well. What do you know?"

"Excuse me?"

"We are going to be best friends. I'm so glad."

What to say to a remark like that? Kelly had no idea. So she didn't say anything.

Finally, the blonde let go of her hand.

Mitch said, "Crystal was just leaving."

Crystal ignored him and spoke to Kelly. "I'm moving to town. I need a new start. And since Mitch needs me here now, everybody wins."

"How many ways can I say this?" Mitch raked an impatient hand back through his hair. "I do not need you."

The blonde acted as if he hadn't spoken. She grabbed Kelly's hand again and pulled her down onto the couch with her. "This is how it is. In L.A., I had a great job working for the wife of a studio exec as her personal assistant. But then, three days ago, he asked for a divorce. She felt forced to downsize. So as of now, I'm in what you might call a state of flux."

"Flux?" Kelly repeated.

"Flux. Mitch and I used to date."

"Really?"

"We met when I was working at Saks. In men's watches. He bought that nice Pasha de Cartier he's wearing right now and he asked me out. And then, when we'd been dating for a couple of months, I had the dream—well, it was more of a *numinous* realization, really. It came to me that Mitch is not the man for me. The energy's all wrong, the stars are not aligned, whatever. What Mitch is, is my brother."

"Of course, I'm not her brother," Mitch insisted. "Crystal, if you need a job, I can get you something at the L.A. office."

"Oh, but he *is* my brother," said Crystal. "My friend, my brother. And I don't want to work for my brother. No thanks, Mitch." She beamed at Kelly. "I love him with all my heart. We keep in touch, being family and all. You know, phone calls or lunch or something, at least once a week. But then he heads off on his supposed book tour and I hear nothing. I call. He doesn't call back. I start getting worried. Finally, Monday, he picks up the phone. He tells me that he's staying here, that he has a daughter and he needs time with her, to get to know her, to make up for all the years of her life that he's missed. The minute I hung up from that conversation, I just knew I was going to be needed here, big-time. And then, Tuesday, what do you know? Suddenly, I'm out of a job. That was when I decided to sublet my place and move to Sacramento."

Mitch blew out a hard breath. "Kelly, she's not staying. Crystal, if you need money, I can—"

"I have my own money, thank you," Crystal

blithely interrupted. "Enough to get by for a while, anyway. But I am going to need a job soon. Not to mention someplace to stay." She glanced at Kelly, a wistful kind of look. "I guess, until I find a place, I'll have to check in to a hotel or something…."

"There's a daybed in the room I use as an office," Kelly said automatically. "You'd have to share a bathroom with our daughter, DeDe, but—"

"Hell, no," Mitch interrupted. "She's not staying here."

"Mitch." Crystal playfully pouted. "You wound me. Deeply. I'm here for you—and you're kicking me to the curb."

He grunted. "Look. If you just *have* to stick around overnight, I'll get you a hotel room."

Crystal stopped pouting. She looked at him steadily. "It doesn't matter what you do. Or what you say. I'm moving to Sacramento—partly for your sake. But also for me."

"This is insane. You don't know anybody here."

"I know you. And now I know Kelly."

"You just met Kelly. And I'm only here temporarily. I mean it, Crystal. This is a bad idea."

Kelly didn't care much for his attitude. How did he know what was right for Crystal? And though the other woman seemed a little flaky, well, so what? And was Kelly gullible? Maybe. But she bought that there was nothing romantic going on between the blonde and Mitch. Which meant that her own admittedly unreasonable jealousy wouldn't have to be an issue.

And really, why did Mitch get to decide who would stay where?

"Your choice," she said to Crystal. "The daybed and the bath down the hall you get to share with a nine-year-old, or some gorgeous luxury hotel suite provided by your honorary brother here?"

Crystal let out a laugh as musical as her speaking voice. "You talked me into it. I'll stay here."

DeDe adored Crystal on sight. She was just sure that anyone so fairy-princess beautiful must be in movies.

"Uh-uh," said Crystal. "I'm way too shy to be an actress—and, Kelly, don't look at me like that. I *am* shy—at least when it comes to getting up in front of people and pretending to be somebody I'm not."

DeDe laughed and grabbed Crystal's hand. "Come on. You like Aly and AJ?" DeDe named her favorite pop stars.

"I love Aly and AJ."

"You look kind of like Aly, you know that?"

"No way."

"Yeah, you do. Come on. I've got the video for *Potential Breakup Song*. I'll show you what I mean…."
DeDe dragged their guest off down the hall.

Mitch and Kelly were left standing in the kitchen.

Mitch said, "Seriously. I'll get her a hotel room."

"Not unless she wants one. I'm perfectly happy to have her stay here."

"First order of business," Crystal said as they lingered over breakfast the next morning. "I need an apartment."

Kelly waited for Mitch to start arguing with her. But no. Aside from looking kind of grim, he seemed to have accepted that his honorary sister refused to go away.

"I'll go with you, to look," Kelly volunteered. "I mean, if you want company." After all, it was Saturday. And Mitch would be around to keep an eye on DeDe.

"Great," said Crystal. "I'll just make a few calls and set up some appointments. I have a good feeling about this. I'm going to find my new home today, I just know it."

Mitch passed her the classified section of the *Bee.* "Knock yourself out."

Crystal rolled up the paper and hit him on the arm with it. "Don't be so cranky. It's not the least attractive."

DeDe appeared in the door from the dining room, wearing her tropical-print swimsuit under a pair of jeans. She had her purple coat over her arm and a swim mask complete with snorkel engulfing the top half of her face. Candy limped over to her and wagged her tail hopefully.

DeDe gave the dog a pat. "Dad. Come on. I'll be late for swimming."

"I'm ready." Mitch got up from the table. He sent Crystal a frown. "You'd better move your car."

Crystal's smile was big and bright. "Did that last night."

Mitch glanced from Crystal to Kelly and back to Crystal again. Kelly thought he was going to say something. But he only shook his head and followed DeDe out through the laundry room to the garage. Candy trailed behind them.

As soon as the door to the garage clicked shut, Crystal said, "God. He's totally in love with you. And not dealing with it well at all."

Kelly sipped her coffee and watched the old dog wander stiffly back in from the laundry room. "I doubt that." Candy limped to her corner and collapsed on the floor with a heavy doggy sigh.

There was a silence. Kelly longed to confide in this "sister" of Mitch's, but she'd only met the woman yesterday.

Crystal spoke again. "I just want to say this. I get that it's really none of my business. Except that I do love Mitch and I want him to be happy. And I think he maybe could be happy. With you. He's mentioned you, to me, in the past. In a…veiled kind of way."

Kelly set down her coffee.

Crystal asked, "You want me to stop?"

Kelly blew out a breath and slowly shook her head.

So Crystal continued. "Whatever happened, when you were together, it was everything to him. He really loved you. A lot. And when he lost you, it almost killed him. He blames you, totally, for dumping him."

"But I didn't dump him. And he knows I didn't. He made that choice. He's even apologized to me for the way he behaved then. He really seemed to mean it, to see that he'd asked the impossible of me. Until I told him about DeDe."

"And suddenly he was blaming you all over again. Hmm. Almost as if he'd never really forgiven you in the first place."

"You think?"

"Hey. That's for you and him to work out."

"We're not working out much of anything, to tell you the truth. He doesn't want to get back together with me. He's made that way clear."

Crystal rolled her eyes. "Which is why he's living in your house?"

"He's only here for DeDe."

"Oh, yeah. Right. I'll leave that alone for now. But you. You're in love with *him,* aren't you?"

"Crystal, I really don't—"

"Aren't you?"

"Fine. Okay. Yeah."

"You want to try again with him?"

"It's not going to happen."

"But do you?"

"God."

"Do you?"

"Yes. All right. I do. Yes."

"And, of course, you've told him what you want."

"Would you not give me that look, please?"

"Hah. So you haven't told him. He doesn't know how you feel."

"There's no point in telling him. He doesn't want to get back with me."

"You don't know that."

"I do. I know that."

"How?"

"I can just tell, that's all. He's not…receptive to me. He doesn't trust me."

"Just tell him you love him. You might be surprised."

"And I might get hurt even more than he's already hurt me. No, thanks. And seriously. I don't want to talk about this anymore."

"I just hate to see the two of you like this. It hurts my heart."

"Crystal."

"Hmm?"

"Enough."

Crystal went through the ads for apartments and made some calls. Then they went out looking. Kelly drove since Crystal didn't know the area.

The third place they went was a walk-in. A sign on the lawn outside the complex advertised a one-bedroom for lease.

Crystal announced, "This is it," before the manager even let them into the vacant apartment. The manager unlocked the door and pushed it inward. Crystal stepped over the threshold. "I knew it," she said. "This is the one."

The apartment, on the ground floor with a view of a nicely landscaped central courtyard from the picture window in the living room, was painted sky-blue. The bedroom had its own fenced patio.

"I am going to love it here." Crystal turned in a circle in the middle of the living room and laughed that beautiful laugh of hers.

The manager led them outside again and showed them the laundry room, the complimentary gym, the rec room and the pool area, which was on the far side of the courtyard. Surrounded by a decorative black iron fence, it was visible from Crystal's soon-to-be living-room window.

"We keep the pool open year-round," the manager said. "It's heated from October through May."

"Excellent," said Crystal.

They moved on to the office, where Crystal signed a lease agreement and wrote a check for two months' rent, plus deposit. Crystal got the keys.

She tossed them in the air and caught them. "Let's go back to my place, just to look. One more time."

So they returned to the apartment and sat cross-legged on the Berber carpet in the empty living room.

"Spacious," said Crystal, grinning at the bare blue walls. "And I do love the blue. It'll be like living in the sky."

Kelly agreed. "It's great. And you are clearly a woman who knows how to make a decision."

"Now, I need a job. I'll start looking Monday."

"Maybe I can help. Depending on what kind of work you plan to be doing."

"I knew you would say that. And I do appreciate it."

"But how about your furniture? Won't you have to go back to L.A. for it?"

"I told my sublet she could have it until the lease runs out. I'll have to make do for the next six months. A couple of futons—one for a couch, one for the bedroom, maybe a table and chairs from Pier 1, to start. I don't mind going minimalist for a while."

"I've got some lamps and side tables up in the

attic you could use. Oh, and some old dishes and pots and pans…"

"See? I'll be set up and ready to roll before you know it."

Kelly's purse started playing Bach. She got out her cell phone, flipped it open and mouthed "Mitch," when she saw who was calling. "What's up?" she asked into the phone.

"You think you could come on home now?"

Alarm jangled through her. "Of course. But why? You sound strange. Has something happened?"

"Kelly, I'm sorry…."

"Oh, God…"

Crystal's amber-brown eyes darkened with concern. "What?" she whispered, reaching out.

Kelly caught her hand and held on. Tight. "DeDe. Is it—"

"No. Settle down. Not DeDe. She's in her room. She's fine. For the moment. She doesn't know."

"Mitch, what are you saying? She doesn't know what?"

"It's the dog."

"Candy? Is she sick?"

"She's gone."

"You mean…?"

"We got home just now and I sent DeDe in to change out of her wet suit and I came in the kitchen. I found the dog lying here in her usual

spot in the corner. She looks really...peaceful. I
think she just—"

"Mitch. What are telling me?"

"Kelly. Damn it."

"What are you saying?"

"I'm saying that your dog is dead."

Chapter Twelve

DeDe sat on the kitchen floor with the old dog's head cradled in her lap. Kelly sat down beside her.

DeDe petted the unmoving black head. "We went to the Ice Cream Factory, Dad and me, after swimming. I had grilled cheese. And even dessert, Rocky Road in a sugar cone." A tear dribbled off her chin and fell to the dog's dark coat. "I prob'ly should have come home sooner."

Kelly put her arm around her daughter and pressed her lips to her chlorine-scented hair. "Naw. Remember? We talked about it. How she's so old. How she would be leaving us soon…"

A sob caught in DeDe's throat. She turned her head into Kelly's shoulder and Kelly wrapped her close. "She seemed okay, didn't she, Mom? She seemed the same as ever today…" More sobs shook her small frame.

Kelly stroked her hair. "She did. She really did." She caught her daughter's sweet face in her hands. "Listen." With her thumbs she wiped away tears, though it did little good, as more tears followed. "Are you listening?"

DeDe sniffed and nodded and sniffed again.

A tissue appeared in Kelly's line of vision. Crystal. Hovering close.

Kelly took the tissue and wiped DeDe's wet cheeks. "I think it was good. The way she went. A good way to go. Just sleeping. Here in her corner…"

"Oh, but, Mommy—" DeDe asked the question all children ask when facing the impossibility of death "—why did she have to go at all?"

"Because she was old. And her body was so tired. She needed a rest. A forever kind of rest."

"Like Grandma Lia?"

"That's right. Like your grandma."

"Do dogs go to heaven, too?"

"Well, what do you think?"

DeDe nodded with enthusiasm. "I think yes. And I think that if any dog should get into heaven, it should be Candy. She was a good dog."

"Yes, she was."

"She loved us."

"She did."

"I loved *her*. I'm going to miss her so much."

"Me, too."

"And I've been thinking…"

"What, honey?" She guided a swatch of tan hair behind DeDe's ear.

"I want to make her a nice grave in the backyard. I want to call Uncle Tanner and have a special…well, not a funeral, but kind of like a funeral. I want to do that today, just us…" She glanced from Kelly to her father, who sat at the table. "And then, maybe tomorrow, we can find a tree or a bush or something to plant in the spot where we put her."

Kelly had been planning on cremation. "Oh, honey…"

"Mom. Please. There's that place back by the fence with no grass on it and no flowers right now. And a little tree would fit there just fine…."

Kelly took another tissue from Crystal and wiped her own eyes. "Honey. Really, I think it's better if we take her to the vet."

"Oh, Mom. No. Please. I want her here, with us. I think she would like that. I really do."

Mitch, who'd been quiet until then, said, "Kelly."

She turned and looked at him. He tipped his head toward the back of the house.

Crystal said, "You two go on. Talk it over. I'll stay here with DeDe and Candy." She got down on the floor on the other side of DeDe. "Okay?"

DeDe sniffed and nodded and kept petting the dog, as if her love and care might bring the old animal back to life.

So Kelly rose and followed Mitch down the hall to his room. He ushered her in ahead of him.

"All right," she said, dabbing her eyes as he closed the door. "What?"

"What can it hurt, to do this the way DeDe wants it?"

She blew her nose, wiped her cheeks. "Mitch. She's nine. Kids that age get unrealistic ideas."

"What she wants sounds pretty reasonable to me."

"Not if it's illegal to bury an animal on a city lot—which I believe it is."

He arched a brow at her. "Are you sure?"

"Sure enough."

"But you haven't called animal control or anything, have you?"

"Exactly what are you getting at?"

"Look. What's to stop us from going with a 'don't ask, don't tell' policy here?"

"Mitch—"

"No, wait. Listen. We would dig down good and deep, so no other animals would come sniffing around. And we'd bury the dog without a box or anything. Decomposition should happen pretty quickly."

"Ugh. Is all that supposed to be reassuring?"

"I'm only saying that it would mean a lot to her, if we buried the dog instead of taking it away to be disposed of at the vet."

"They do cremations. We could have her ashes…."

He gave her a patient look. "Think about it. Think about that tree. Hey. It's always a good thing to plant a tree."

She let her shoulders slump and shook her head. "I just don't know."

"Come on. It's a small enough thing, to give DeDe the closure she needs on this."

"Closure. Right. Poor old Candy is dead. That's closure enough, it seems to me."

"Say yes. In the end, you'll be glad that you did." He reached out and brushed a tear from her cheek. Her whole body warmed at the simple caress. She wished he hadn't done that.

She wished he would do it again. "Oh, all right."

He didn't smile, exactly—or maybe he did. But just with his eyes. "Good. I think it's the right decision."

"I'm not so sure—but thanks."

"For?"

"Not taking her side against me in front of her. Especially at a time like this."

He did smile then. "Hey. I'm learning. I'll be a good dad before you know it."

"You are a good dad, Mitch. You honestly are."

"Well. I'm working on it."

She thought about how they really did need to get down to an agreement on the length of his stay in her house. They needed to tackle the big issues of how they would share custody, of where DeDe would live and when.

And he needed to go back to his own life and quit being a constant reminder of all she would never share with him.

"Ready?" He had his hand on the doorknob.

She swallowed and nodded. "Let's go."

Tanner came right over. He and Mitch dug the grave. Then Mitch carried the dog out and laid her body gently in the cool, dark earth.

They stood around the open hole in a semicircle, wearing their jackets against the winter cold—Crystal and Tanner, DeDe, Mitch and Kelly.

"Before we cover her up," said DeDe, "I just want us to say the things we loved about her." She sent Kelly a questioning glance. Kelly nodded in reassurance. "Okay, then. I'll start. I loved how she came to us, just showed up one day to live with us. Even though I don't remember it, exactly, 'cause I was too little, I love that she did that, that she found us. She wasn't young then. And someone had hurt her. She had scars in her coat and torn up ears and she walked with that limp. But she kept trying. I always think of it like she'd been looking and looking for just the right family. And we were it. We loved her and cared for her and she looked after us."

Kelly went next. "Candy was easy to have around. She never messed in the house or chewed up the furniture. If you told her to go lie down, she went right to her corner. But she was affectionate, too."

"Oh, yeah," said DeDe, remembering with a smile through her tears. "She would bump your hand to get petted, and she would follow me anywhere if I only called her name. And if I would get sick, she would lay down on the floor by my bed and wait for me to get better."

Tanner said, "She had that funny bark."

Crystal laughed. "I heard that bark. Like it took all the oomph she had in her to get it out."

Mitch said, "She didn't shed a lot. Did she?"

And DeDe said, "Oh, Dad." She looked around at the semicircle of mourners. "Well. I guess that's enough." She shivered and hugged herself, her breath a puff of fog on the cold air. "I just wanted her to know that we did love her. Lots and lots." She picked up a big handful of dirt and tossed it in.

"There. I saw them do that on TV…" She glanced from Mitch to Tanner. "Okay. Please put the dirt back in now."

Mitch and Tanner grabbed their shovels.

Kelly, Crystal and DeDe waited in silence until the job was done.

Once they were back inside, DeDe said, "I think I want to go watch the Disney Channel for a little while…."

Kelly gave permission and she headed for the family room. "Stay for dinner?" she asked Tanner.

"Can't." He finished washing his hands at the sink and reached for a towel. "I'm on a job. I took a break for this, but I have to get back…."

Kelly walked him out, as was her custom.

"I think she'll be okay," he said as they went down the driveway toward the beige sedan he often used when he was working.

"Yeah. She seems to be dealing with it pretty well, actually."

They reached the sedan. He leaned against the driver's door and folded his arms over his chest. "So. That Camaro. Must be the blonde's, huh?" Crystal had left her car in the driveway when they returned.

"Yep. And her name is Crystal, by the way."

"I know her name. You did introduce us."

"Tanner. I like her. A lot."

"What? Is that a warning?"

"Just so you know. You don't have to run a background check on her or anything. She's a good person."

"You know this already, after…what, a day?"

"Yeah. You can scoff all you want. I know she's a good person. I just do. And I mean it. Do not check up on her."

"Okay, okay. So what's her story?"

"She's a friend of Mitch's from Los Angeles. Moving to Sacramento. In fact, she signed the lease on an apartment today."

"Got all that. She have a job here?"

"She's going to get one and I'm going to help her with that. I swear, you are terminally suspicious."

"Yeah, well. I'm suspicious for a living. And look at what's happening here. You've got Mitch moved in on you and now some L.A. blonde. I don't want to see you get taken advantage of."

"Tanner. Stop. *I'm* the one who invited Crystal to stay here. And she's not staying long. She'll be moving to her new apartment sometime in the next couple of days."

"And Mitch?"

"What about Mitch?"

"How long is he staying?"

"I don't know yet. Not long."

"Kelly. He's been here for two weeks."

"So? I explained all this to you. More than once."

"Are you getting back together?"

"We've been through all this. I've told you. No. We're not getting back together. He just needs some time with his daughter, okay?"

"You're mad at me."

"I'm not."

"Kell. If you're in love with the guy, maybe you ought to just—"

"I didn't say that. Did I say I was in love with him?"

"You should see your face."

"I don't want to talk about this."

He put up both hands. "Hey. All right. I'm done. I won't bring it up again."

They stared at each other. She thought how dear he was, how he only wanted the best for her. "You're my big brother and you always want to protect me, to make everything okay for me. But with this…you just can't. It's my problem to work out. And Tanner, I promise you, I will work it out. In the end, I'll be fine, whatever happens. And DeDe will be fine, too."

"Kell?"

"What?"

"You can stop convincing me. I believe you."

"Well, then. Okay. Good."

"It's only that sometimes, I…" The words trailed off.

"Sometimes you…?" she prompted.

He squeezed her shoulder. "Forget it. As long as you're all right."

"I am. Truly."

"Gotta go." He turned, pulled open the car door and slid in behind the wheel. "Sorry about the mutt."

A pang of sadness touched her heart. Candy. Gone. She would be missed. "Yeah. Me, too. She was a sweetie."

The next day, Mitch took DeDe out and they found a dwarf maple. The dinky tree was hardly more than a Y-shaped stick with a root ball at the end. Then again, if you looked close, you could see the tiny leaf buds like little knots on the delicate twin branches. They planted it together, father and daughter, with Kelly and Crystal looking on, above the spot where Candy rested.

Monday, Crystal bought her futons and a small table with two chairs. She had them delivered to her new place on Tuesday. Mitch rented a pickup and that evening they took over the things Kelly had given her—kitchen stuff, a few tables and lamps, some linens and a chest of drawers. Crystal moved in to her apartment that night.

And the next morning she started looking for a job.

Thursday made it three weeks since Mitch had moved in. Kelly knew she had to talk to him. She was growing much too accustomed to having him around day-to-day.

And so was DeDe.

They counted on him. Both of them, in the ways you count on the family members who live with you. It wasn't wise.

It wasn't…right.

Kelly found she was even getting used to wanting him and not having him. Lord. Was that normal?

Scary, but it had started to feel as if it was.

And that made her sad, somehow. The idea that she could slowly come to accept wanting him desperately and having him right there—where all she had to do was reach out and touch…

But she wouldn't.

She couldn't.

It had to stop.

It wasn't right.

Friday night, DeDe had a recital at the dance academy and a sleepover at her friend Mia Lu's afterward. They drove to the studio in Mitch's Lexus, Mitch and Kelly in front, DeDe in the back. Like a family.

Which they were, in a way. They both belonged to DeDe, and she to them. But not to each other.

Never to each other…

She glanced at Mitch behind the wheel. He sent her a smile.

Fake, she thought. Not real. She had to remember that. She couldn't let herself be lulled into imagining they might work things out.

They let DeDe off in front to go get into her first costume and then parked around back. They walked side by side, as if they really were together, to the main entrance of the academy's performance hall. Kelly, who'd brought a tray of cookies, lingered in the lobby to help the other moms get the refreshment tables ready for after the show. Mitch went on into the auditorium and pitched in with setting up the rows of folding chairs.

About fifteen minutes before the program started, Mitch and Kelly took their seats. A few minutes later, Crystal appeared. She took the chair on Mitch's other side. Not long after, Tanner arrived. He sat by Kelly.

One big happy family.

More or less.

The good part, as always, was watching DeDe perform. No, she didn't have much dancing talent. But she sure had a fine time up there on that stage.

After the recital, the adults surrounded her and told her how wonderful she was. She beamed at their praise. They all hung around for cookies and punch. Tanner mentioned he had an out-of-town job to deal with. He'd be gone for the next week, which meant he'd miss the usual family Sunday dinner. Kelly hugged him and told him to keep safe.

Around nine-thirty Crystal and Tanner headed for their cars and DeDe transferred her sleeping bag to Eve Lu's van. She climbed in back with the other girls and off they went.

That left Kelly and Mitch. Alone. Together.

They drove home. To Kelly's house. Where Mitch lived as if it were his home, too.

The ride was mostly a silent one.

Except for the usual surface talk, centering around their daughter.

"DeDe looked great tonight," he said.

She agreed. "I wish I'd brought my camera. I left it on the kitchen counter and then walked right past it…."

"One of the other mothers will have some shots with her in it."

"That yellow daisy costume in the second number. I'd give anything for a picture of her in that." The parents helped make the costumes, but then they always donated them to the academy for use in future productions.

"Borrow the costume if you have to," he suggested. "I'm sure the academy won't mind."

"Yes. Good idea. I might just do that."

At home, he headed down the hall—to his room, she assumed. Kelly lingered in the kitchen. She put the water on for some tea and sat at the table and tried not to look at that empty spot in the corner where Candy liked to sleep.

"Miss that dog of yours, huh?" He was standing in the doorway from the dining room, wearing the same khakis and sweater he'd worn to the recital.

She felt…a glow all through herself, just to look at him. A glow and a sadness. At what would never be. "Yeah. I keep thinking I see her in the corner of my eye. But then I turn and look. Nothing. An empty space."

"It's a common reaction."

"I know. Still hurts, though."

"DeDe seems to be doing all right, dealing with it."

So. What was happening here? Kelly wasn't sure. Maybe he was lonely. She could relate to that. She felt lonely, too.

She confessed, "I think you were right. About letting her bury Candy, about going with her wishes and helping her plant that tree. I think she feels that she did all she could to honor the pet she loved. And that's kind of…empowering for her."

He slanted her a look. "Empowering, huh?"

"What? Is that the wrong word for it?"

"No. It's just…."

She suggested, "One of those words they use in self-help books? Like *closure* and *self-esteem*."

"Exactly."

She couldn't help teasing, "I believe you mentioned *closure* yourself not so long ago...."

"Guilty as charged." He nodded toward the stove. "Your water's boiling."

It seemed only civil to offer. "Want some tea?"

"I'd take a beer."

"Go for it."

He went to the fridge and she went to the stove. It was...homey. Nice. Seductive in its very warmth and simplicity: Mitch and Kelly, puttering around the kitchen, like old married people.

Except that they weren't and would never be married.

Married.

Just thinking the word made her heart ache. All those years ago, when they were kids, they'd both been so sure they would live happily ever after, the two of them.

Until death do us part...

He popped the top on a bottle of Corona and sat at the table again. Brewing the tea took her a little longer.

But soon enough she joined him. *Keep it light,* she thought. A little friendly and totally casual conversation. What could that hurt? "I keep meaning to tell you I read your book. I really liked the chapter on how every success is created twice—first in the mind and heart, in careful detail and then in the real world."

He shrugged. "It's old stuff. But I put my own spin on it."

"That's how you made your millions—by creating your companies in your own mind, making a mental blueprint of them before you ever tried to make them happen in real life…."

"Billions," he corrected with a grin. "It's how I made my billions."

She chuckled. "Right. Billions. A million bucks is not what it used to be."

"Sadly, no—and maybe the book makes it look a little too easy. There was a whole lot of fumbling around, stumbling blindly in the dark. And there were big disappointments. A whole lot of failures, of getting it all wrong."

"Still. What you've accomplished in ten years. It's pretty astonishing."

He seemed to study her. "You're a damn fine mother," he said after a moment.

The words were complimentary. The tone, not so much. "And that makes you angry?"

He frowned. "Yeah. I guess it does, at least a little. She's a great kid and I had nothing to do with it."

"You resent that."

"Can you blame me?"

Things were straying a little too far from the light and the casual. Still, she answered him honestly. "No. I don't blame you for feeling cheated."

He almost smiled. She had the sense of an argument narrowly averted. "Well, okay then. And I mean it. You've done a great job with her."

"Thank you."

"Somehow, she believes in herself and her place in the world absolutely. But without being a jerk about it, without being a brat. She's confident, and at the same time, she has a big heart. She's responsible, amazingly so for a kid of nine. She does her homework and her chores around the house before she asks to watch TV or play Super Mario."

"You're right. She's a good kid. And I'm more than happy to take all the credit."

He raised his beer and drank. She found herself watching his Adam's apple, imagining putting her lips to the side of his strong neck, scraping the skin there with her teeth….

Her breath snagged in her throat and, down low, she felt the heat of desire.

Ignore it, she thought. *You want him. So what? It's old news.*

He set the beer down. They shared a look. Too long, too deep. Much too arousing…

And then he stood. She thought he would leave her, go on back down the hall. She told herself that would be good—at the same time as she had to stop herself from begging him to stay.

But he didn't go. He came toward her. He held out his hand.

She looked at his open palm, longing moving through her, as hot as a day in midsummer, thick and sweet as slow-poured honey. "Oh, Mitch. No…"

"You don't mean that. Take my hand."

"We agreed we wouldn't—"

"I agreed to nothing. You sent me away, because of DeDe. I understood that. But DeDe's not here tonight. Whatever we do will be just between us." He kept his hand outstretched to her.

"You say that. But it goes nowhere. It's not what I want."

"You're lying. You do want it. You want me the same as I want you. I can see it in your face, in your eyes. In the softness of that mouth of yours. In the way you're breathing—shallow and fast. Take my hand."

She tried to remember all the reasons she should keep saying no, should get up and leave him, head straight for her room.

But he was right. She did want him. And now, tonight, she couldn't refuse him—didn't want to refuse him. She reached up. His fingers closed over hers.

Pure heaven. The warmth of his skin, the strength in his grip.

He gave a tug. It was all the encouragement her

yearning body needed. She surged up and into his waiting arms.

"This is…bad," she whispered, and breathed in the heady, masculine scent of him. What was it with that? Why did no man in the world smell as good as him? "We shouldn't do this."

His eyes were dark as the middle of the night. And every bit as seductive. "I want you. I always want you."

"I don't—"

"Shh. Don't say it."

"But—"

"Just kiss me. We can take it from there."

"But I—"

His mouth brushed hers. Fireworks. Magic. "Say yes…."

It was too much. Her body burned. She was on fire. For him. She heard herself say the word, "Yes…" It came out muted, almost unformed.

Because his mouth was already covering hers.

Chapter Thirteen

"My room," he whispered. And then he was kissing her again.

She kissed him back, her body melting, and somehow, at the same time, on fire. She wrapped her arms around his neck and fused her mouth to his.

He explored her, one hand curving down over her hip, while he slipped the other under her shirt. She moaned at that, at the feel of his hands on her, caressing her. He stroked the skin over her rib cage, then cupped her breast through the barrier of her bra.

He wasn't content with that. Oh, no. He eased his

fingers up and inside the bra cup. He caught her nipple between two fingers.

"Oh," she moaned against his open mouth. "Oh, yes. Anything…"

"Everything." He said it low. Rough. "All of you…" Those words scraped a hot caress along every nerve.

And then he wrapped both arms around her and lifted her feet off the floor. She kicked, backward. One shoe dropped off and then the other. He stepped around them and carried her—kissing her deeply, her legs dangling loose—across the dining room, down the hall and through the open door to his bedroom.

He lowered her to the rug beside the bed, grasped her waist—and set her away from him. She tried to sway toward him, tried to press her hungry, yearning body back against him.

But he didn't allow that. "I want to see you," he commanded. "All of you. I have to touch you…" He started undressing her as he spoke. Quickly. With fierce efficiency, he took off her sweater and tossed it away. "Help me…."

She didn't argue. She felt the same urgency he did, to be open to him, to be completely revealed. She reached behind her and unhooked her bra, letting it slip down her shoulders, pulling it off and tossing it toward a chair as he moved in close again.

He encircled her with those big arms of his—in order to unbutton her skirt and slide the zipper down. She moaned in excitement as he shoved her skirt over her hips.

"Step out of it," he instructed gruffly. She did. And then he was tearing at her pantyhose, ruining them in his haste.

Not that she cared. She helped him, hooking her thumbs under the elastic waistband, shoving at them, wiggling those pantyhose down. All the way. She braced herself on his shoulder, lifting each foot in turn, getting them off, wadding them into a ball. She gave them a toss toward the wastebasket.

Did they make it? She didn't bother to check.

Finally, she was naked. The way he wanted her. She pulled at his shoulders, moaning, urging him to stand again, to envelope her in his embrace, to give her his hard, strong body to lean on.

But he was on his knees by then and not getting up. He pressed his face to her belly, nuzzling, moving lower.

She clutched his dark head as he kissed the curls that covered her sex. He moved lower and she felt his warm breath on her hidden flesh. She opened for him, tipping her head back on a moan as he tasted her deeply.

Her knees were weak. And the bed was right behind her. Such a simple thing, to back up that extra step. He stayed with her, never once breaking that deep, purely sexual kiss.

She sat. He continued kissing her, easing her legs even wider apart and putting his palm flat against her belly, urging her to lie back, to surrender her body completely to him.

No problem. No issue. Whatever he wanted. Okay. Fine. Absolutely right.

With a deep, surrendering sigh, she lay back across the bed. He clasped her ankles. She took his cue and lifted her feet to rest them on his shoulders. His expensive sweater was silky soft, the muscles beneath hard and hot.

She was spread wide for him and he took full advantage. She didn't mind in the least. She clutched the comforter and called his name as he kissed her so deep and so thoroughly.

It only took a few minutes of such arousing, concentrated play and she hit the peak, sliding over into ecstasy with a glad, triumphant cry. He stayed with her, drank from her body as her pleasure claimed her.

Did she pass out with the joy of it, with the sensual intensity of her release?

She couldn't have said.

But the next thing she knew, he was rising above her, his khakis wide, his manhood jutting proudly, more than ready for her. He'd already prepared himself with the condom.

"Mitch…" She lifted her arms to him.

"Scoot back, on the bed…."

She did as he commanded, and he came down to her. She took him into her, hooking her legs around the backs of his thighs.

Oh, the wonderful hard, strong weight of his body on hers….

Was there anything in the whole world so glorious, so purely male as that? To feel him at the core of her, finding her, then sliding deep.

She took him. All the way.

He pressed his mouth to her temple. She turned her face, scenting him, reaching to taste his kiss again.

His mouth touched hers. At last. The kiss they shared then swept her away—the marvelous play of tongue on tongue, the warm press of his lips, open on hers, the slick heat within…

She lifted her legs even higher and hooked her feet around his waist. They rocked together, two parts of the same whole, lost to each other for long lonely years, but joined again, at last, in an endless, amazing, wet glide.

He swept a hand back, caressed her knee, guiding her leg straight so he could change their position. He turned them, so they lay on their sides, facing each other, still joined.

Her eyelids felt deliciously weighted, too heavy

to lift. Still, somehow, she did lift them. She looked into his eyes.

"Good," he whispered as he moved within her. "So good…the best. Always. Kelly…"

"Michael," she said without thinking. He didn't correct her, but she gave him his new name, too. "Mitch…" Just to be fair.

He stroked her shoulder, petted her hair, as all the while they moved together, rocking so sweet and hard and long.

In the end, he rolled again, so that she could rise above him. She folded her legs under her and sat astride him, riding him. Rising, she let him slide out—but not quite all the way. As he moaned his pleasure, she pressed down to take all of him once more.

"Too many clothes," she muttered. "You have too many clothes on…."

He chuckled. "I was in a hurry." And then he groaned when she shoved at his sweater, pushing it up, to give her hungry hands access to the tempting flesh beneath. She stroked his hard belly, bent to lick circles around his tight masculine nipples.

Oh, just to touch him, to feel him within her. Was there anything sweeter than that?

There was. Oh, yes. She realized it soon enough as the pleasure rose within her, spilling out, bursting into ecstasy all over again.

He grabbed her hips and held her to him, lifting his body to give her everything. She felt him pulsing inside her as, moaning her name, he found his completion in tandem with hers.

Kelly cuddled against his chest as her breathing slowed to normal. Eventually, she slid to the side and he got up and got out of his clothes, rejoining her quickly, reaching for her again.

They made love a second time, so slowly and tenderly, both of them wanting to make it last and last.

In time, they got under the covers. She cuddled up close to him, rested her head on his shoulder, settled her hand over his heart.

Really, she thought, not sure whether to smile in satisfaction or frown in disapproval, she had to stop ending up naked around him. It set a bad example, was bound to get him thinking that it was all right with her, to make love with a man who still held the past against her, a man who blamed her for all the years of not knowing that he had a child.

But then again, well, she did love him. She truly did. Somewhere between that other night when he'd ended up in her bed and now, she'd made her own private peace with that, with loving him in spite of everything.

She loved Mitch Valentine.

Amazing. Impossible. True.

How long did she intend to put off telling him? What was it Crystal had said?

Just tell him you love him. You might be surprised.

And, well, that was the problem, wasn't it? That she might be surprised in a really bad way.

But even her brother, who still had reservations about whether Mitch was the man for her, seemed to think she ought to go ahead and take a chance, show him what was in her heart.

Even if he still claimed he didn't love her, well, he might at least give her hope for the future. It did seem that he'd begun to see more than the past when he looked at her, that he might be getting to the point where he could stop blaming her for not searching for him hard enough, for not finding him sooner.

The ten years they'd lost were gone. They would never get them back. Why throw away the next ten?

And the ten after that?

"Mitch?" All of a sudden, her mouth was dust-dry. She had to swallow.

"Hmm?" Lazily, he stroked the outside of her arm with the back of a finger. Lovely shivers followed in the wake of that caress.

She lifted up on an elbow, so she could meet his eyes.

Did he seem…guarded?

A little bit wary, maybe?

Or was that only her own cowardice talking,

whispering doubts in her ear, so she'd keep her love—keep the truth, keep her heart—to herself?

He touched the side of her face. "You drive me crazy, you know that? You always did. I see you and I want to touch you. And when I do touch you, I only want to touch you some more."

She cleared her throat. "Well. That's good. Right?"

"It's excellent." He combed her hair back with gentle fingers, guiding it along her temple, tucking the strands behind her ear.

She dared to ask. "Do you think, maybe, there could be more?"

He frowned. Was that a bad sign? "More?"

She gulped. And threw caution out the window. "I love you, Mitch. All over again. So much. I want…to be with you, to be together. To make a family—you and me and DeDe. Like we always dreamed when we were kids."

He said nothing. He lay very still.

"Mitch. Please. I need to know. Is there a chance for that? A chance for you and me."

He looked straight in her eyes and he said, "No."

Chapter Fourteen

Kelly sat up, clutching the sheet to her breasts. She pulled away from him—to the far edge of the bed.

Mitch had to actively resist the urge to reach for her, to grab her back into his arms. Why the hell did she have to go and bring love into it? Why couldn't she have just left it, let things go on as they were? Why did she find it necessary to complicate the issue this way?

He sat up, too. "Look. I thought I made it clear—"

"Oh, yeah." She spoke softly, but he could hear the tremor in her voice as she strove for control. "You made it clear, all right. You don't like me. You don't trust me. You just want to live in my house and have sex with me whenever our daughter's not around."

"That's not so."

"What do you mean? Of course it's so."

"Listen." He couldn't stop himself. He went ahead and reached for her.

"No." She batted his hand away. "Don't. I mean it. Just…don't." She hugged the sheet to her body. "I…" Her blue eyes brimmed. But no tears fell. She blinked them away. "So. All right. Got my answer, didn't I?"

He said nothing. He didn't know what he felt right then. Anger, maybe? Frustration? Hurt…

And guilt.

Yeah. All right. He felt guilty.

He knew that this—taking her to bed—wasn't right. It wasn't…good.

There was too much between them. He wanted her. He wanted his child.

But…

He just couldn't forgive.

He couldn't love her, never again. And the stupid idea he'd had that they could enjoy each other without consequences, well, look how great that had turned out.

Time to get things straight, clean up his damn act. He met her gaze dead on. "All right. I get it, okay? I'm way out of line here."

"Oh, no kidding…"

"And I'm sorry. Sincerely. But I just can't go there with you again. I can get past your leaving me when we were kids. But that you had DeDe and didn't move heaven and earth to find me…I *can't* get past that. I'll never get past that."

"But you still want to have sex with me? *I'm* sorry, Mitch. I find that just plain cruel."

She had it right. He knew it.

She said, "And that brings us to the real question, the one you keep putting off. You have to know. I can't have you living here anymore. Not after this, after you've made it unbearably clear that there's no hope for the two of us, ever. Not now, when I'll have to know every time I look at you that you made love to me when you *knew* there was no hope for us. It just…it hurts way too much. You have to…go back to your own life. You have to let me go back to mine."

"Yeah." He said it quietly. "I know."

She lifted the blankets and swung her legs to the floor. He looked away, denying himself the beauty of her nakedness. He heard her go into the bathroom and then return a moment later.

"When, Mitch? I need to know when you will go."

He turned his head her way again. She stood by the bed. She'd wrapped herself in one of the bathroom towels. "Tomorrow," he said. "After DeDe gets home. I'll talk to her. Then I'll leave."

"Fair enough." She grabbed her scattered clothes and started for the door. But after a couple of steps, she turned back to him. "I have to say this…."

He knew that whatever it was, he wouldn't like it. Too bad. After the way he'd just treated her, he owed it to her to hear her out.

She said, "I just don't get it, Mitch. I don't understand. I did love you when we were kids. I don't think you have any idea how much. You killed me when you made me choose the way you did. And then, when I couldn't find you because you just disappeared, well, it was as if you'd killed me again. And what about now, Mitch? Look at you now. With your fancy new name and your buffed-up body and your billions, with your corporations and your book deals and your inspirational speeches. You're the definition of *success* now. You *are* the American Dream, aren't you, Mitch? But you know what? You haven't really changed at all. I look at you and I still see the same bitter, unforgiving boy who made me choose between him and my brother ten years ago. I don't know why I keep loving you. God. I wish I didn't."

Mitch had one of those nights. All alone with his guilty conscience and his dread of the morning.

When he'd have to tell his daughter that he was leaving.

He rehearsed what he'd say endlessly. He tried not to recall Kelly's parting words, tried not to acknowledge the truth in them. And he tried to ignore her scent on the sheets, tried not to see her face every time he closed his eyes, tried not to long for the touch of her hand, the feel of her body moving beneath his...

The morning came, all sunny and bright with the promise of spring. He'd be leaving Kelly's house on a beautiful day.

Leaving to go...where?

L.A.? Dallas? He needed to check in at each of the offices, but both corporations had been performing well in his absence. It didn't really matter where he went first.

It didn't really matter....

How grim was that?

It was time, he'd been thinking for several months now, to move on, get started on something new. He had a few ideas on the back burner. He would choose one to focus on. Start making plans, fooling around with where he might take it.

The scent of fresh-brewed coffee kind of snuck up on him. So. Kelly was up.

But he found the kitchen empty. She'd propped a note against the coffee machine.

Going to Crystal's. I'll be back by eleven, after you've talked to DeDe. In time to say goodbye.

Good, he tried to tell himself. Better that she'd left. It wasn't as if they had any more to say to each other.

And he was not, under any circumstances, going to let himself imagine what she would say to Crystal….

"I'm all for healthy eating." Crystal set the plate of doughnuts on the table. "But sometimes you just need a nice big helping of sugar and saturated fat."

"It's so hard to choose," said Kelly. "They all look so good." She grabbed a chocolate-covered old-fashioned and took an enormous bite.

"Am I right or am I right?" asked Crystal.

Kelly chewed and swallowed. "I feel better already." She gobbled down some more of the delicious, sinful treat.

"I also give a mean hot-rock massage."

Kelly only grunted and stuffed her face with the doughnut.

Crystal said, "I could talk to him."

"No!" Kelly said the word around a mouthful of sweet dough and then had to stop long enough to swallow. "Absolutely not. I just want to get over him. Again. I just want to get on with my life."

"But you love him and—"

"He doesn't love me. Period. End of long, sad story—and do not say that he does love me, he just won't admit it. As far as I'm concerned, if that's the case, it's the same as if he didn't love me at all."

"He's a jackass." Crystal blotted up sprinkles from the plate and licked them off her finger. "I love him forever. He's the brother I never had. But still. He's a jackass."

"I couldn't agree with you more."

"Have another doughnut."

"Don't worry. I intend to. I'm not leaving this apartment until I've gained ten pounds."

"That's the spirit."

Kelly didn't feel all that spirited. She just felt like crying. And then crying some more. "Maybe I ought to be there, when he talks to DeDe."

Crystal gave her a steady look and a shrug. "Totally your call."

"But no. I said I'd be back at eleven. I'll stick with that. It's his thing and I need to stay out of it." She put her head in her hands. "Tell me that I'll get over this."

"You will. I promise you. Though I totally get that it doesn't feel like that now."

"Oh, Crystal. It hurts so much."

Crystal leaned across the table and offered her hand. Kelly took it. The contact helped. Utter despair subsided into a dull throb of misery.

* * *

Mitch went through the motions of a normal morning. He fried himself a couple of eggs, sat down with his food and coffee and the *Bee*.

But the newsprint all blurred together. He kept seeing Kelly's face, when she told him she loved him. So full of hope. And fear that he would turn her down.

Which he had immediately done.

No. It was for the best. He needed to put her from his mind. He focused on the sports page.

Time dragged. But eventually, ten o'clock approached. At quarter of the hour, he left to get DeDe.

She babbled the whole way home, about the recital and how well she thought it had gone, about the sleepover and how she'd stayed up 'til past midnight. "And, Dad, I'm not the least bit tired."

He stared through the windshield and thought about how he was going to make himself tell her that he was leaving. Right away. That the next time she saw him, it would be at one of his houses. For a weekend. Or a holiday. Or—

"Dad. You're acting funny."

He glanced across the console. DeDe wore a worried frown.

He forced a smile. "Sorry." And he turned his eyes back to the road.

At home, she grabbed her pack and he took her sleeping bag. He followed her in through the laundry room, admiring the bounce in her step. She was such a happy, well-adjusted kid.

Damn. He dreaded this.

When they reached her room, she went on in and tossed her pack on the bed. He lingered in the doorway, lowering the sleeping bag to the floor.

"I had fun," DeDe said. "But it's good to be home."

Damn it to hell, where to even start? "DeDe."

"I should put away my stuff. Where's Mom?" She started unzipping the pack.

"Over at Crystal's. She'll be back soon. Listen. DeDe." He stepped into the room and caught her small hand before she could start pulling stuff from the pack.

She looked up at him, worry darkening her wide eyes all over again. "Dad?"

He pushed the pack aside. "Come on. Sit down."

"Um. Okay." She jumped up on the bed.

He sat beside her. "Remember the day you asked me if I was your dad?"

She bobbed her head with great enthusiasm. "Oh, yeah. It was in the limo, right after I told John that he was a good driver."

"Yeah. And that night, we talked about your coming to live at my house part of the time."

"And I 'splained it to you. How I can't do that. How you needed to live here."

"And so I stayed. So we could get to know each other better."

She put her small hand on his arm. He looked down at her perfect little fingers and he knew absolutely that he could not do this. She said, "I'm glad that you decided to live here with us. Aren't you?"

"DeDe. I don't live here. I've just been… staying here. For a while, so that you could get to know me better before you came to live with me part of the time."

She snatched her hand from his arm. "No. That's not right. I can't live somewhere else. I live here. At my house."

"DeDe—"

"Dad. Listen. You live here, too. You bought a TV for your room. And a desk and all that stuff. You live with us now."

"No. I don't live here."

"You do."

"DeDe, I don't. You have to accept that."

"No. No, I won't. No. No, no, no…" She was shaking her head frantically, on the verge of an outright tantrum—out of nowhere.

Never had he seen her act like this. She was a good kid. Reasonable. Well-behaved.

He tried again. "I'm sorry that it upsets you, but I do have to leave. Today."

She stopped shaking her head long enough to demand, "Why?"

"It's…time, that's all. I've stayed here for weeks."

"Because you live here!"

"DeDe. Listen to me. You will be coming to see me soon, for a weekend. Or maybe longer. Sometime when you're not in school." She was shaking her head again. "DeDe. Stop shaking your head. Listen to me."

She whirled on him. "No. You can't go. It's not fair. You can't!"

"I am going. I have to go."

"No, see. You don't have to. Never. You don't."

"I do."

Tears filled her big eyes and spilled down her cheeks. "I don't want you to go. You stay here!"

"DeDe…"

"No! No, no, no, no…" She threw herself down on the pillows and sobbed like it was the end of the world.

He had no idea—zero—of what to do next. So he stood. "I'll…be back in. To say goodbye in a little while."

"No, no, no, no…"

"I hope you've calmed down by then."

Did she hear him? He couldn't tell. She sobbed as if she'd never stop and between sobs, she kept crying, "No! No, no, no…"

He backed out of the room and shut the door quietly behind him.

And then, for several minutes, he just stood there outside her door, his chest so tight it ached, wishing he knew how to calm her.

And hating himself for making her cry, for not having the foresight to ask Kelly to be here for this. He glanced at his watch: 10:36 a.m. She'd be back soon. She'd know what to do….

He went to the kitchen and sat at the table and waited. Each minute lasted for an eternity. At least from that end of the house, he couldn't hear his daughter's sobs.

He heard the garage door opening at two minutes to eleven. About damn time.

She entered the kitchen and saw him. "My God," she said. "What?"

"I told her I'm leaving. It wasn't good. She wouldn't listen. She started crying."

Kelly dropped her purse on the counter. "She's in her room?"

He nodded. "She's never going to get over this."

She took a step toward him. But then she caught herself and moved back again. "Mitch. Of course she'll get over it."

"You don't know. You weren't there."

"I'll go talk to her."

"Please. Not that it'll do any good."

With a nod, she left him.

He waited some more. Six full minutes. He knew because he watched the kitchen clock the whole time.

At last, he heard footsteps in the hallway.

DeDe appeared. Her nose was red and her eyes

puffy. But the storm of tears had passed. She hovered in the doorway, looking so small and sad, hanging her head. Finally, she straightened and looked at him. "I wish you weren't going, but Mom says you have to."

There should have been something just right to say then. He didn't have a clue what that might be. So he held out his arms.

"Oh, Dad…" She hurled herself at him. He barely had time to get on his feet before her small body landed against him. He hugged her and she hugged back. "I'm sorry," she whispered. "I'm sorry. I just didn't want you to go…."

He looked down at her shining hair, at her small shoulders and her arms wrapped tight around him, and he longed to stay, to make a life here, with her.

And with Kelly.

If things could have been different…

But they weren't. Some things, a man just couldn't get past. Some things, a man could never forgive.

Chapter Fifteen

Funny, how easy it is for a woman to get used to having a man—the right man—around. How easy to come to count on him.

And not only for the obvious things: ferrying a daughter to her various activities, helping with the dishes, being there to talk to about everyday subjects in the evenings and at breakfast…

More than that. So much more.

Things a woman never thinks of until a man is gone: nighttime, for instance. In bed—and no, not even the feel of him beside her under the covers. Kelly had certainly enjoyed that. But after all, in the weeks that Mitch had lived with her, they'd only shared a bed twice.

Uh-uh. It was…the knowledge of him, there, in the house. His very presence.

Oh, yeah. Knowing he was there. *That* was everything.

He left an emptiness behind, a special place that had been filled with him. With his strength. With his intelligence. With his sense of humor that showed itself often, in spite of a certain darkness in his nature.

Kelly missed him. It hurt so much, to lose him all over again. He left that emptiness in her world, in her house, in her life. As well as a sadness that only time would ease.

He called on Tuesday night. He spoke to her briefly, explaining how he was setting up an account for her and DeDe. It was important to him that they never want for anything. As to a custody arrangement, he'd be getting back to her on that. Maybe they could just play it by ear for a while.

She said that would be fine with her. And they agreed that next month, over Easter, DeDe would be staying with him. He'd come to see the school play, which was right before the Easter break, and then he'd take her to Los Angeles with him for the week she was out of school.

Then he asked to talk to DeDe. Kelly put her on the phone.

Wednesday, Crystal found a job working as a secretary for a small legal firm. She and Kelly met for lunch on Thursday.

Crystal said, "I don't know how long I'll last working there, but it's good to have a paycheck until I can find something more interesting." She said she'd talked to Mitch on Monday. "He called me, but then he got mad when I told him what a jerk he was being. I let him know that he was a fool and I said he'd better get his butt back here to Sacramento where he belongs."

Kelly shook her head. "You shouldn't have."

"Hey. I call it like I see it."

Kelly couldn't resist asking, "And then he said…?"

"That I should stay out of it and he really had to go. I figure I won't hear from him for a while. Eventually, I'll call him. Because I do love him, though sometimes I can't help but wonder why."

"Funny," said Kelly.

Her gorgeous blond friend looked at her sideways. "Not."

"I don't mean him. I'm over him."

"Don't lie. It makes your nose get longer."

"Hah. But I'm talking about you."

Crystal fluttered her long, thick eyelashes. "Well, I always love to talk about me."

"I feel like I've always known you, like we've been friends forever."

"Probably because we have. Past lives, all that."

"Don't go all woo-woo on me, okay?"

Crystal laughed. "You sound like Mitch."

"Who? Never heard of him."

Tanner got back to town Saturday. He called around two in the afternoon, just to check in.

"You don't sound right," he said about forty seconds into the conversation. "What happened?"

She'd meant to keep it calm and reasonable. She honestly had. But something about the love and concern in her big brother's voice really got to her. Or maybe she'd been on the verge of tears for days and refused to admit it.

Maybe both. Who knew?

She started sobbing. All at once, she was crying so hard, she could hardly talk.

Mitch swore. "Where's DeDe?"

"She's…at…the Y." She sobbed. "Swimming…"

"I'm on my way."

He was there in ten minutes. He burst in the door and took her in his big, strong arms and let her soak his shirt with the river of tears that wouldn't stop pouring out of her.

She cried endlessly, sobbing and hiccupping. Eventually, he guided her to the sofa in the family room, handed her a wad of tissues and said, "So. I take it Mitch left."

She blew her nose and wiped her streaming cheeks. It didn't help much. The tears kept on falling. But somehow, between sobs, she told him everything—well, okay, she skipped some of the more intimate details, but he got the gist of it.

"That bastard," he said. "He blames you for not finding him sooner, is that the main point?"

"Y-yes!" She surrendered to a fresh flood of weeping.

"And you've told him, right, that you had me on it the whole time, that you were constantly checking with me, eager to hear if I might have found out anything?"

"H-he doesn't believe me. He thinks I didn't try hard enough. And that you…didn't look."

"Because he's right. I didn't look."

Kelly's hiccup caught on a gasp. "I don't…you what?"

Swear words filled the air. "I made a call I had no right to make, okay?"

"I don't… A call?"

"A decision. I was so damn mad at that guy, for the way he treated you. And then to vanish like that when you really needed him…"

"But you…you *told* me. That you were looking, that you were coming up with nothing…"

"And I did look. For the first year or so. I put a lot of time in, trying to find that jerk. But the months passed and I didn't catch a break. DeDe was born. You were doing okay. I started to think you'd be better off without him. That the best thing that could happen was if he just stayed gone. So I threw his file away. You would ask me if I'd found anything about him, if anything had come up. I would say no. I'd leave out the part about how I had stopped looking."

Kelly put her hands over her eyes. "Oh, Tanner. Oh, no…"

He was silent. He just sat there beside her, waiting.

Eventually, she dropped her hands and looked at him. "How could you?"

He didn't flinch. He regarded her steadily through somber eyes. "Because I thought I knew best. I was wrong. So wrong there aren't really any words for it. And I've been a coward over it, thinking that now you found him yourself, the two of you would work it out. That I'd never have to admit how I screwed him—and you and especially DeDe—out of the chance to be together sooner, out of the years you might have had."

The tears welled again. This time they fell silently, without the fanfare of sobs, just dribbled steadily down her cheeks and plopped on her hands, which she'd clenched tightly in her lap.

He said, "If you're going to hate me now, I guess I understand."

She wiped her eyes. "How can I hate you? You're my brother. I love you. I'm pretty damn mad at you, right now, though. It's going to take me a while to forgive you."

"I understand. And I am sorry," he said bleakly. "So damn sorry. Though I know that does nothing to make things right." He stood. "I can see in your eyes. You want me to go."

She got up, too.

He said, "I'm going to track him down. Have a talk with him like I should have done weeks ago. Set him straight about who's to blame in this mess."

"Do what you want," Kelly told him. "But I don't think that's going to fix anything."

"Damn it, Kell. It wasn't your fault."

"Oh, yeah. It was. Because the truth is, I *didn't* look for him. I put it on you, when I knew how you felt about him. I was mad at him, I was so hurt and angry. That he'd left me, cut me out of his life like a bad habit. That I was having his baby and he was nowhere to be found. I didn't want to have to track him down myself. I just wanted to hand it over to you and have you fix it. And, well, you did fix it, didn't you? You fixed it the best you knew how. So we all had a part in what happened. We all did wrong. Mitch. You. And me, too. I see that now. Too bad it's too late to matter much."

* * *

"Mom, I'm home!" The front door slammed.

"I'm in the kitchen!"

DeDe came through the living room at a run and skidded to stop a feet from where Kelly stood at the sink, peeling potatoes.

"So, how was the swimming?"

"It was good. We did the butterfly stroke. I like swimming." She flipped her wet braid back over her shoulder. "What are we having?"

"Stew."

"Eeeww."

"Stew is good for you. Go on and change out of that wet suit."

DeDe didn't budge. "Mom?"

"Hmm?"

"Are you okay?"

"Fine, honey. Just fine…"

"You're not looking at me."

Kelly sucked in a breath and made herself turn to her daughter. She pasted on a smile.

DeDe shook her head. "Your eyes are all red and puffy. I know you've been crying."

It was no good. Kelly dropped the half-peeled potato, wiped her hands on her jeans and grabbed her daughter in a hug.

"It's Dad, huh?" DeDe held on tight. "You're sad about Dad."

"I am. But I'll get over it."

"Maybe if we could—"

"DeDe." Kelly said her daughter's name firmly.

DeDe got the message. "Well. Never mind."

Kelly took her by the shoulders. "Go on in and change. And come and help cut up the carrots."

DeDe slanted her a look. "Seems like, since we're so sad, maybe we should get pizza tonight or something."

Kids. So resilient. And always ready to work the angles. But what the hey? "I suppose I could save the stew for tomorrow…."

DeDe tried hard not to look too happy about that. "Good idea."

"I still need you to cut up the carrots."

"Be right back." She was off like a shot.

Crystal came for Sunday dinner. Tanner didn't. The three of them—DeDe, Crystal and Kelly— played Wii bowling after they had the stew. Then they ate ice cream.

DeDe went in to take her bath at eight-thirty. Kelly offered tea and Crystal said she'd love some.

"So where's the hunky big brother?" Crystal asked as she drizzled honey into her tea.

"I'm tempted to tell you some harmless lie, about how he's working, about how he just couldn't make it tonight…."

"Never lie to me," said Crystal. "It's bad for our friendship, which is the rarest kind, having lasted through several lifetimes and all. Just tell me you don't want to talk about it."

"I don't want to talk about it. Not right now, anyway."

Crystal nodded. "I so can respect that. Shall I tell you about how much I hate my job?"

"But you just started there."

"What do you have when a lawyer is buried up to his neck in cement?"

"You tell me."

"Not enough cement—I'm collecting lawyer jokes. Humor. It's the only way to get through the day when you work for an attorney."

At nine Sunday night, Mitch sat at his desk in his top-floor corner office in Century City.

The office—well, pretty much the whole building—was deserted. There was, as a matter of fact, no real reason for him to be sitting there, staring blankly at his 40-inch flatscreen desktop monitor, on which was displayed a 3-D prototype for a tabletop electronic interface. The device, which *was* the top of a table, could connect every electronic device a given individual might possibly own. All data and programs could be accessed through it. And since it was completely wireless, it made the usual unsightly cords and cables of a home PC a thing of the past.

The good people at Microsoft already had their own such device in development, but Mitch was considering giving them a run for their money on it….

And was there some pressing need for him to be studying the tabletop prototype on Sunday night?

No. None.

It was, quite simply, better than going home to his futuristic spaceship of a house in Malibu, where he could hear the waves lapping the beach beyond his bedroom balcony and ponder such universal mysteries as why he'd managed to end up alone.

Again.

He missed his kid.

And he missed Kelly. Bad. Worse than before…

He couldn't even call Crystal and take her out to dinner and listen to her woo-woo chatter and feel… connected in spite of himself to another human being. She lived in Sacramento now.

One of the red lights on his desk phone lit up: the security desk downstairs. He punched the speakerphone button. "Yeah?"

"Mr. Valentine, I've got a Tanner Bravo down here to see you."

His pulse exploded into overdrive. *Kelly,* he thought. *DeDe.* Had something happened? Were they…?

But no. If there had been an accident, he would have gotten a call, not a sudden visit from Tanner. Of all people.

And how, Mitch found himself wondering, had Tanner known to look for him here, at his L.A. office after nine on a Sunday night? For a guy who had never managed to find Mitch in ten years, Tanner had done pretty well at getting to him now.

Why?

One way to find out. "Send him up." He hit the speaker button to turn off the phone and then got up and went to meet Kelly's brother at the elevator.

The elevator doors slid open. Tanner wasted no time on chitchat. "We need to talk."

"This way." Mitch led the other man down a couple of corridors, past long rows of darkened work cubicles, to the open door of his office. He stepped back so Tanner could enter first. "Have a seat."

Kelly's brother shook his head. "This isn't the kind of thing I want to tell you sitting down."

"Yeah?"

"We should be facing each other. That way it'll be simple for you to pop me a good one."

Mitch came even with Kelly's brother. They stood several feet from his black granite desk. "All right. Here we are."

Tanner said, "I never liked you."

"You came all the way to Century City to tell me what I already know?"

"When Kelly found out she was pregnant with DeDe and we couldn't find you, I swore to her I would track you down."

"I know all this."

"I'm not finished. For a year or so, I did look for you. I worked at it pretty hard, as a matter of fact. But as time went by, I started asking myself why the hell I should be looking for a man who'd made it so damn clear that he didn't want to be found. So I tossed your file in the trash and I stopped looking. I lied to Kelly and told her I was still trying. Whenever she would ask me how the hunt for you was going, I'd give her details, tell her all about how I was busting my butt trying to find you, I'd even make up leads that then would always peter out to nothing…" Tanner paused, arched a black eyebrow. "So. Wanna hit me yet?"

"You're saying Kelly really did believe that you were looking? You're saying you outright lied to her for years."

"That's right. I thought she—and DeDe—would be better off without some guy who cared so little, he walked away without looking back, some guy who put in a lot of effort never to be found. I thought, why should I find *him?* He doesn't even want it. And Kelly and Deirdre are doing just great without him."

Mitch did want to punch Tanner's lights out. He wanted it a whole lot. But somehow he held himself in check. "You tell her what you did?" Tanner nodded. "And she said…?"

"She's mad as hell as at me. But she doesn't blame me. Not any more than she blames herself. And you. She says we were all at fault. Me, for not lookin', her for turning the job over to me—and you for running away, for not being there when she needed you the most."

Mitch swore.

"Go for it," said Tanner.

Mitch's fist shot out and made contact. Tanner grunted as his head flew back. He landed hard on the buffed concrete floor.

Mitch reached down and gave him a hand up. "You all right?"

Tanner tested his jaw. "Yeah. Okay. I got a few questions."

"Fine. Ask."

"When you gonna let all this bitterness go? When you gonna come for your family? When the hell you coming home where you belong?"

Mitch stood at the floor-to-ceiling windows behind his desk for a long time after Tanner left. He stared out at the endless blanket of lights that was the city at night and thought about the things Kelly's brother had said.

It was all wrong. All of it. Especially his own part in it. Was the situation salvageable? After all the time he couldn't forgive her, would Kelly ever be able to forgive *him* now? He had his doubts.

Finally, he turned off his computer and left the office, dreading the empty Malibu house, but knowing he had nowhere better to go.

In the lobby, where he had to switch elevators, there was a lot of racket going on.

Doug and Deke, the two security guys, were chasing a mutt around the security desk. It was a pitiful-looking scrawny brown thing, collarless, coat all matted, tongue lolling. It scrabbled on the marble floor, slipping and sliding—but somehow managing to evade capture by the guards, who were laughing as they tried to corner it.

"That's it," panted Doug. "You got him…."

Deke let out a shout as he lunged for the dog, who somehow managed to slide around him to freedom once more.

"What's going on?" Mitch asked the two guards—as if it wasn't painfully clear.

"Mr. Valentine!" The two men snapped to attention as the dog slipped away again and headed for a corner, where it wiggled in behind a potted palm.

Panting, Doug explained. "Deke went down the

street to Starbucks." He gestured at the two tall coffee cups waiting at the desk. "Somehow that mutt slipped in when he came back. We're just trying to get him so we can put him out again."

Over by the potted palm, the dog had dropped to its skinny haunches and sat watching, eyes alert, tongue still hanging out. The animal actually looked as if it understood every word that Doug was saying. It let out a low, hopeful whine, soulful brown eyes locked on Mitch.

Mitch didn't know exactly what came over him then. "I'll take care of him."

Deke and Doug blinked in unison. Deke started to protest.

But Doug elbowed him in the side. "Well, fine. I mean, if you want to."

"Thanks," said Mitch, who had no clue in the world what he was going to do with an ugly, dirty mutt—given that he could catch it in the first place. "Enjoy your coffee." He nodded at the men.

They went back behind the high desk and Mitch was left facing the ugly dog, wondering what he should do next.

"Okay," he said to the mutt. "Here, boy." He said it with no hope that the dog would respond.

But damned if that animal didn't go back up on all fours and wag his mangy tail.

"I'm leaving now," Mitch said conversationally.

"If you want to come, you're just going to have to follow." He slapped a hand against his thigh and commanded, "Here, boy," again.

The dog trotted right over. You could count the ribs beneath its dirty coat. The poor thing smelled like a hairy ball of garbage.

Stray, Mitch thought. He knew how that felt. "I cannot believe I'm going to let you in my Mercedes."

The dog whined again, one tattered ear cocked high.

"Ever been to Malibu?"

The dog just looked at him. Deke, behind the counter, snorted back a laugh.

"Let's go, then." Mitch nodded at the men and slapped his leg again.

The dog followed right behind him.

"Tony Moroco is coming to San Francisco." Renata sipped her coffee. The full-color brochure for a program called *Discover Your Total Power, Now!* lay spread wide on the breakroom table in front of her. "He's amazing." Renata put her hand to her heart. "And those cobalt-blue eyes of his. Absolutely mesmerizing…" She took her hand off her heart and fanned herself with it. "Hot, I tell you. Smo-kin'!"

Kelly filled her cup with coffee and sat opposite

Renata. "I swear. If a guy's got a plan for self-improvement, you're all over him."

Renata gave one of her gusty sighs. "Oh, yeah. There's something about personal empowerment in a man. All that enthusiasm. All that endless positive energy. I could have an orgasm, just reading this brochure."

Melinda, the receptionist, poked her head in the door. "Kelly. Visitor."

"Does my visitor have a name?"

"Mitch Valentine."

Renata gasped. "No way!"

Kelly was thinking pretty much the same thing. Somehow, she managed to give Renata a nod as she pushed herself to her feet. Damn. Her legs were shaking. "I'll, um…see him in my office. Give me two minutes and then show him in."

Somehow, she managed to wobble down the hall and into her private space. She hovered at the door, debating—should she shut it? Leave it open?

She shoved it closed and staggered around behind her desk. Sinking gratefully into her chair, she put her head in her hands and let out a moan.

What was he doing here? What did he want now?

A tap at the door.

She popped up straight, folded her hands on the desk pad and cleared her throat. "Ahem. Come in."

The door swung open.

It was Mitch, all right. He wore khakis and a polo shirt and he'd never looked so good.

"Hello, Mitch."

He stepped into the room and shut the door. "Kelly."

"Something I can do for you?"

He gazed at her for a long time. Too long. Until she could feel her face flushing and her mouth trembling and she wanted to shout at him, to order him to get out, to leave her alone. How could she get over him if he wouldn't go away and stay gone?

Then he said, "I love you. I've always loved you. You are my heart and my life. You're all that's worth living for. I'm here to find out what I need to do to get you to give me another chance."

Kelly knew she couldn't have heard right. "Wh-what did you say?"

He winced. But he did say it again—more or less. "I love you. I want to try again. Will you? Please?"

Joy burst wide inside her. She quelled it. She just didn't trust him, couldn't let herself believe him. "Excuse me," she said softly. "But how can you try again when you never tried in the first place?"

A muscle in his square jaw twitched. "You're angry."

"You're damn right I'm angry. What are you doing here?"

"I told you. I—"

"You left me. Twice. Broke my heart so bad both times... I can't even tell you how bad you hurt me."

"God. Kelly. Please..."

She was not going to cry. She was not. "It's Tanner, right? Tanner came to see you."

"He did. Yeah."

"And now you know I actually did try to find you, suddenly that makes it all fine for you? You're willing to forgive me?"

"Kelly, come on..." He took a step closer.

She put up a hand. "No. Stay right there. Listen."

He stopped. "What? Tell me. Anything...."

"It's...it's not like that, okay? Not all clear and defined. I was so mad at you, back then. Madder than I am now, if you want the hard truth. Mad and hurt so deep down I thought I'd never get over it. But I was having your baby. I knew I had to find you. When you weren't at the trailer park and no one knew where you'd gone, I turned it over to Tanner. And when he didn't get anywhere, did I challenge him? Did I tell him, look, I'm going to find someone else, someone with no personal involvement, to take up the search? No. I did no such thing, you understand? Because I was *still* bitter and angry at you—just like you've been at me. Deep in my heart, I was so busy being hurt at your desertion, that I lost sight of the main point—which was to get you home to your daughter, no matter the cost to myself and my poor, battered heart.

"So the years went by. Enough of them that I began to believe you would never be found. I was a lot more resigned to that idea than I should have been. By the time I saw your picture in the paper last month, I'd long ago accepted that my daughter would never know her father, just like I never knew mine."

A silence.

At last he said, "Is that all?"

She made a scoffing sound. "Isn't that enough?"

He asked, "Can you...do you still love me?"

She said, "Damn you, Mitch."

"Do you?"

"Did you hear what I said? Do you understand what I just told you?"

"Kelly, I get it. It's okay. I get why you did what you did. You're at fault. I'm at fault. We're all at fault—well, except for DeDe. I know it's hard for you to believe me, but I want...your forgiveness now."

"*My* forgiveness. You're the one who couldn't forgive."

"You're right. I couldn't. I told myself it was all your fault. You had chosen your brother over me. You hadn't looked hard enough, hadn't really tried to find me. You'd *stolen* my daughter from me..."

"So given all that, I'll ask you again. Why are you here?"

"I see now that was all wrong."

"No. No, you weren't wrong. I did choose Tanner over you, I *didn't* look hard enough for you and as a result, in a way, I did steal your daughter from you. I stole the years you should have had with her."

He shook his head. "But there's a deeper truth."

She blinked. "There is?"

"That's right. The truth is that none of those things would have happened if I hadn't turned my back on you in the first place. And that's what I couldn't forgive, Kelly. That's what I could never get past."

She got it. "Yourself. You haven't been able to forgive yourself."

"Not only that, I blamed you as a way to keep from facing how bad I'd screwed everything up. I was ready, before I knew about DeDe, to accept my responsibility, to apologize to you for the choice I forced on you, to go on from there. But when I heard you'd had my daughter…it was just too damn terrible. I couldn't deal with it."

"And now?"

"I've done the worst. I've turned you away for the second time. I got back to L.A. and…I wondered what the hell I was doing there. Over the days since I left you, the truth has been creeping up on me. That visit from your brother kind of brought it all into focus. Damn. I want to get past this, finally. Once and for all. I don't think I'm quite ready to forgive myself. I don't blame you if *you* can't forgive me. But, well, I want to get on with our lives—if you can, I mean, after the rotten way I've treated you. If you…still want to be with me the way that I want to be with you."

"Oh, God." She gulped, hard. She swallowed the tears away. It was no time for crying. It was the moment for hard truth. "A week and a half ago, I said I loved you. I asked you then to try again with me. You looked at me and you just said no."

"Kelly…" He came closer.

She popped to her feet. "You have no clue how hard that was for me to do."

He came around the desk. She turned to confront him. He said, "Kelly. I know. I do."

She opened her mouth to argue. But then she remembered the words of love he'd said to her only moments ago. She couldn't deny that his coming here, his telling her he loved her, now, when she so easily could have hardened her heart against him… that couldn't be easy.

Let alone his admitting at last that the person he needed most to forgive was himself.

"Give me a chance," he whispered. "Just one chance. It's the only one I'll ever need. I'll make good on it, I promise. I'll give you everything."

Was she a fool to believe him? After all the bitterness, after all that had gone wrong, was she out of her mind to give him that chance he was begging for?

Oh, yeah.

But that chance he wanted…?

She wanted it too. She wanted it bad.

She challenged, "You will stay with me this time?"

"I swear it."

"You will never walk out on me again, no matter how tough it gets?"

"Never."

"You will love me and our daughter. And take care of us and…treasure us?"

"Beyond anything. Above all."

"I am not playing around here, Mitch. This is a forever kind of thing. We will be married. We will be a family. Once you take this step, there's not going to be any turning back. Are you sure you're up for that?"

"I am. It's all I want. All I dream of."

"Oh, Mitch. Look what you've done now. I'm actually starting…to believe you."

"Good," he said fiercely. "Believe me. What I tell you now is true. I love you. I've always loved you. I've done a really bad job of it, I know. I've never loved you the way you deserve to be loved. But I'm ready now, Kelly. To be the man you need. The man you can count on. The man you marry. The man to stay by your side. For the rest of our lives."

"Oh, Mitch…"

"Come here. Come on…" He reached out those big arms.

And she went to him. He gathered her close, held her so tight.

"I must be crazy. But I love you, too," she whispered. "I still love you, in spite of everything…."

"Prove it. Kiss me."

She lifted her mouth to him, eagerly, hungrily.

Oh, it was wonderful. The absolute best kiss she'd ever shared with him. A kiss of hope. A kiss free of doubt or anger. A kiss that promised a lifetime.

Together.

When he lifted his head, she said, "I think you should do that once more."

He didn't argue. He kissed her again.

The next time they came up for air, he asked, "Do you think you could take the rest of the afternoon off?"

"I think I could arrange it."

"We could pick up DeDe from school, tell her we're getting married."

"Married." Kelly laughed. "I like the way you say that."

"Let's go."

She grabbed her purse and turned for the door.

He hung back. "Uh, there's one more thing you should know."

Her stomach tightened. "What? Okay. Now you're scaring me."

"In the car...?"

"Yeah?"

"There's a dog."

She stared at him. And then she laughed. "You went out and got a dog?"

"Well, not exactly. The dog kind of got me."

"A stray?"

"That's right."

"Oh, Mitch...yes."

"Yes, a stray is good?"

"A stray is terrific. DeDe will be so happy. What's her name?"

"It's a he. And he doesn't have a name, really. I've been calling him 'boy.'"

"Don't worry. You know that DeDe will be more than willing to give him a name." She reached for the doorknob. "Well. Are you coming?"

"Oh, yeah." Three long strides and he was at her side. He took her hand. "I'm right here."

They stopped in the breakroom and Kelly introduced him to Renata, who was quite flustered, yet still managed to tell him how much she'd learned from his book. He promised to autograph a copy just for her.

They went on to the front desk, where Kelly told Melinda she was taking the rest of the day.

"Family leave?" asked Melinda.

Kelly shared a smile with Mitch. "Family leave. Exactly."

And they went out together, holding hands, into the bright sunshine of the first day of spring.

* * * * *

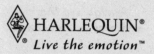

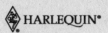

HARLEQUIN *Super Romance*®

Bundles of Joy—
coming next month to Superromance

Experience the romance, excitement and joy with 6 heartwarming titles.

BABY, I'M YOURS #1476 by *Carrie Weaver*

ANOTHER MAN'S BABY
(The Tulanes of Tennessee)
#1477 by *Kay Stockham*

THE MARINE'S BABY (9 Months Later)
#1478 by *Rogenna Brewer*

BE MY BABIES (Twins)
#1479 by *Kathryn Shay*

THE DIAPER DIARIES (Suddenly a Parent)
#1480 by *Abby Gaines*

HAVING JUSTIN'S BABY (A Little Secret)
#1481 by *Pamela Bauer*

Exciting, Emotional and Unexpected!

*Look for these Superromance titles in March 2008.
Available wherever books are sold.*

COMING NEXT MONTH

#1885 THE SHEIK AND THE PREGNANT BRIDE—
Susan Mallery
Desert Rogues
When mechanic Maggie Collins was dispatched to Prince Qadir's desert home to restore his Rolls-Royce, she quickly discovered his love life could use a tune-up, too. Qadir was more than game, but would Maggie's pregnancy shocker stall the prince's engines?

#1886 PAGING DR. DADDY—Teresa Southwick
The Wilder Family
Plastic surgeon to the stars David Wilder, back in Walnut River and the hospital his father once ran, was on a mission of mercy—to perform reconstructive surgery on a little girl badly injured in an auto accident. Would Courtney Albright, the child's resilient, irresistible mother, cause him to give up his L.A. ways for hometown love?

#1887 MOMMY AND THE MILLIONAIRE—Crystal Green
The Suds Club
Unwed and pregnant, Naomi Shannon left her small town for suburban San Francisco, where she made fast friends at the local Laundromat. Sharing her ups and downs and watching the soaps with the Suds Club regulars was a relaxing treat…until gazillionaire David Chandler came along, and Naomi's life took a soap opera turn of its own!

#1888 ROMANCING THE COWBOY—Judy Duarte
The Texas Homecoming
Someone was stealing from Granny, ranch owner Jared Clayton's adoptive mother. So naturally, he gave Granny's new bookkeeper, Sabrina Gonzalez, a real earful. But forget the missing money—a closer accounting of the situation showed that Jared had better watch out before Sabrina stole his heart!

#1889 DAD IN DISGUISE—Kate Little
Baby Daze
When wealthy architect Jack Sawyer tried to cancel a sperm donation, he discovered his baby had already been born to single mother Rachel Reilly. So Jack went undercover as a handyman at her house to spy. Jack fell for the boy…and for Rachel—hard. But when the dad took off his disguise, all hell broke loose.…

#1890 HIS MIRACLE BABY—Karen Sandler
To honor his deceased wife's wishes, sporting goods mogul Logan Rafferty needed a surrogate mother for their embryos. Her confidante Shani Jacoby would be perfect—but she was his sworn enemy. Still loyal to her best friend, though, Shani chose to carry Logan's miracle baby…and soon an even bigger miracle—of love—was on their horizon.

SSECNM0208